"Whatever the position is, I'm sure I can do it. I'm very adaptable," Orla said, getting ahead of herself again.

"I'm happy to work a probation period, as long as I can keep working with our horses," she added a little frantically, the leap of desperate hope sparkling in her deep green eyes.

Desperate was good, eager to please even more so—it made her all but perfect for the role he had in mind. Except...

Karim let his gaze drift over her slender frame again, the boyish clothes, the lack of makeup and the wild hair now beginning to curl around her ears, and still felt the inexplicable ripple of arousal that had surprised him in the stables, annoyingly.

"What job did you have in mind for me, Mr. Khan?" she asked.

"I want you to become my fiancée, Ms. Calhoun."

USA TODAY bestselling author **Heidi Rice** lives in London, England. She is married with two teenage sons—which gives her rather too much of an insight into the male psyche—and also works as a film journalist. She adores her job, which involves getting swept up in a world of high emotions; sensual excitement; funny, feisty women; sexy, tortured men; and glamorous locations where laundry doesn't exist. Once she turns off her computer, she often does chores—usually involving laundry!

Books by Heidi Rice

Harlequin Presents

Bound by Their Scandalous Baby
Claiming My Untouched Mistress
Claimed for the Desert Prince's Heir
A Forbidden Night with the Housekeeper

Conveniently Wed!

Contracted as His Cinderella Bride

One Night with Consequences

Carrying the Sheikh's Baby

Passion in Paradise

My Shocking Monte Carlo Confession

The Christmas Princess Swap

The Royal Pregnancy Test

Visit the Author Profile page
at Harlequin.com for more titles.

Heidi Rice

INNOCENT'S DESERT
WEDDING CONTRACT

HARLEQUIN®
PRESENTS®

Recycling programs
for this product may
not exist in your area.

ISBN-13: 978-1-335-40337-7

Innocent's Desert Wedding Contract

Copyright © 2021 by Heidi Rice

This edition published by arrangement with Harlequin Books S.A.

For questions and comments about the quality of this book,
please contact us at CustomerService@Harlequin.com.

Harlequin Enterprises ULC
22 Adelaide St. West, 40th Floor
Toronto, Ontario M5H 4E3, Canada
www.Harlequin.com

Printed in U.S.A.

INNOCENT'S DESERT
WEDDING CONTRACT

To my sister Nemone

Thanks for taking me to my first ever racehorse auction. Who knew it was so grand!

H x

PROLOGUE

'WHY DON'T YOU just find yourself a wife, bro? That'll stop the old goat trying to force you into an arranged marriage.'

'No, thanks, *bro*,' said Karim Jamal Amari Khan, Crown Prince of Zafar, sarcastically as he knocked his brother Dane's booted feet off the coffee table, which his interior designer had probably paid a fortune for. 'Our father can't force me to do a damn thing.'

'Father's a rather loose term, don't you think?' Dane flashed a smile so sharp it could cut concrete. 'Seeing as his only participation in our upbringing was to get both our mothers pregnant?'

'True but irrelevant,' Karim lied smoothly. As the older son and nominal Crown Prince, he had been subjected to rather more attention from their father—including the horrendous summers he'd been forced to spend in Zafar after his mother's suicide. Summers Dane knew nothing about. 'The point is I have no desire to acquire a wife for our father's benefit. If he wants to disinherit me, he can.' In fact, Karim would be overjoyed at the prospect. The kingdom of Zafar held nothing but bad memories for him, which was precisely why he had carved his own path, building a billion-dollar business empire from the ground up by the age of thirty-two, and had not been back to the kingdom since the summer he turned sixteen.

'Which would leave me in the firing line,' Dane replied, the sharp smile taking on a rueful tilt. 'Gee thanks, bro.'

'Tough.' Karim chuckled. It would serve his father right to end up having to declare Dane his heir. His younger brother was reckless and undisciplined and had even less interest in their family heritage than he did. While Karim's mother, Cassandra Wainwright, had been a young British aristocrat, who had returned to the UK with him after the divorce and sent him to a series of tediously disciplinarian boarding schools, Dane's mother, Kitty Jones, had pursued a jet-set life as New York's premiere wild child after her divorce. And her son had reaped the whirlwind, living a life with no boundaries whatsoever. There were only four years between them but Dane had refused Karim's offer to join Amari Corp as an executive and set up his own hospitality brand five years ago, which had been surprisingly successful. If there was one thing Dane knew how to do, it was throw a party.

'I know something which might change your mind about acquiring a wife, pronto,' Dane said, the wicked glint in his eyes making Karim uneasy. There was nothing Dane enjoyed more than messing with him—which had to explain why he had turned up unannounced at Karim's mansion in Belgravia at eight this morning, after a red-eye flight from New York.

'Which is?' Karim asked impatiently, deciding to cut to the chase. He needed to start work, so he didn't have time for his brother's little joke.

'The old goat knows you're after the Calhoun stud,' Dane said as if he'd just scored a home run.

'How do you know that?' Karim demanded. His pursuit of the Calhoun stud was top secret.

Michael Calhoun had died nearly a year ago leaving the family's horse-racing bloodstock and training facility in Ireland with crippling debts. They'd sold a lot of their stock to stay afloat but he'd discovered a few days ago the business was finally being forced to go in to voluntary liquidation. And Karim had been preparing to go in for the kill as soon as it went up for auction.

'Overheard it at an event last night in Tribeca from one of Dad's many mistresses. Which was why I caught the last flight out. She told me he was…' Dane lifted his hands to do air quotes '…real thrilled about getting involved in racing by buying Calhouns. Which we both know is code for he plans to screw you over on the deal to force your hand on the marriage front.'

Karim swore under his breath.

'A phone call would have sufficed,' he murmured, knowing his brother's primary reason for catching the red-eye was probably to see him sweat in person. He refused to give him, or his father, the satisfaction. 'But thanks for the heads-up,' he added grudgingly.

He would have to lose the deal.

Which would hurt like hell. The Calhoun facility, even depleted and without Calhoun himself at the helm, represented a chance to enter the world of horse racing and build his own legacy—something he'd been planning for a while. The only thing he had enjoyed in Zafar was riding and training his father's Arabian stallions.

But he refused to engage with his father's games, on any level. The old bastard had pulled similar tricks in the past, forcing Karim to go head to head with him. Karim hadn't cared, in fact he'd enjoyed finding ways to best the bastard at first. To show him that he wasn't

scared of him, that he had no power over him
any more. And as he'd built his business, it had
become easier to win. But as his father's attempts to blackmail him became more desperate, more deranged, he had become aware that
every battle was taking a toll on Zafar's econ-
omy as well as his father's finances. Once one
of the richest kingdoms in the region, Zafar was
losing prominence because his father had been
syphoning off money to spend on this war of
attrition. Karim might not feel any connection
with his heritage, but he didn't want to see the
country's citizens punished. So, several years
ago, he'd stopped engaging with his father—
by keeping the deals he was involved in secret,
or bowing out if his father showed an interest.
It had taken a few strips off his pride, but he
knew the non-engagement technique was working—his father hadn't been involved in any of
his business in over a year. Ultimately, frustrat-
ing the bastard was more important than beating him, as it wasn't his father who would pay
the price.

'Why not call his bluff, this time?' Dane said
forcefully. 'Instead of dropping the deal.'

'I'm not getting married to close a deal...'
Karim said, wondering if his half-brother had
lost the plot.

'But what if you weren't *really* getting married?' Dane cut in. 'Why not acquire a wife in name only?' he continued. 'It would be the perfect revenge on the manipulative bastard. If you're not sleeping with her, you can't provide him with the heirs he wants.'

'And how would that work, exactly?' Karim snapped, annoyed now with Dane's nonsense. 'The main reason I do not wish to marry has nothing to do with our father. I simply do not want a wife.' He slept with women, he did not have long-term relationships with them. 'Even a fake wife would expect things… And make demands on my time.'

And could become as weak and needy and fragile as his mother.

He resisted the shudder as the memory of his mother's tear-stained face flitted across his consciousness. His mother's sadness had defined his childhood, he was not about to become responsible for another woman who needed things he could not give her.

Which was why he had a nicely appointed four-bedroom mews cottage in Kensington where he kept the woman he was currently sleeping with so she would be available when he wanted her, no messy emotions required. Maybe the place had been empty for a month— he frowned—or even two. But since paying off Alexandra, when she had begun to make noises about 'something more permanent', he simply hadn't had time to acquire another mistress.

'Bro, you're loaded,' Dane replied, with that charming, concrete-cutter grin.

It occurred to Karim, while his brother enjoyed messing with him, Dane liked to mess with their father a great deal more.

'Get your fancy legal team to put together an iron-clad prenup,' his brother continued. 'Then all you've gotta do is find yourself a woman who is greedy or desperate enough to be bought.'

CHAPTER ONE

'ORLA, ORLA, THERE'S a helicopter circling the farm. Gerry just gave them permission to land on the back pasture. Gerry says it's *him*, the sheikh who's going to put us all out on the street.'

Orla Calhoun paused while mucking out Aderyn's stall at her sister Dervla's panicked shout. The sleek black stallion jostled her as he shuffled his hooves. She pressed her hand to his nose, to soothe him. Unlike most retired racehorses, Aderyn was placid enough for her to muck him out while he was still in the stall. He liked the company, almost as much as she did, but even so…

'Shh, fella, it's okay, she's just stressed,' she whispered, before leaving the stall. She propped the rake beside the stall, latched the stable door, whipped off her work gloves and glared at her sister. 'For goodness' sake, Dervla, how many times have I told you not to raise your voice around the horses?' she hissed. 'You could spook them and someone could get hurt, or, worse, the animal could get hurt.'

They only had six horses left now, but each one of them meant everything to her—and she still mourned the loss of the horses they'd been forced to sell in the last year. Each one unique, with a personality and a purpose that had always meant more to Orla than just winning races or accruing stud fees. Perhaps that was why she had ultimately failed in her attempt to keep Calhouns going, not because she hadn't been good at training and caring for the horses, but because they had always meant more to her than just a business.

And now she was going to lose it all…

'All right, all right. I get you,' Dervla whispered back, grabbing her elbow to drag her away from the stall, and not sounding all that apologetic. 'But what are we going to do about *him*?'

Orla heard it then, the sound of a helicopter powering down. It was far enough away not to disturb the animals, but the sound would never be quiet enough not to disturb her.

'Are you sure it's him?' she asked. 'He's not due here till Friday.'

The liquidator had arranged to have Crown Prince Karim Jamal Amari Khan view the facility before the auction on Saturday. This must be a preliminary visit by one of his minions. Sure, it had to be. She wasn't ready for him.

She glanced down at her work boots and dirty jeans, the sweat-stained camisole that clung to her breasts. She'd been up at dawn to take Aderyn out on the gallops and had been mucking out the stalls ever since, because they'd laid off the last of the stable boys almost a month ago.

'Gerry said he spoke to him,' Dervla whispered. As if the man was standing behind them. 'He's piloting the helicopter! He came on his own, Gerry says.'

The anxiety that had gripped her stomach ever since she'd been forced to face the inevitable took another vicious twist.

She'd had a plan to have the house and herself spotless when he arrived. When you were going to beg a favour from a playboy sheikh, you needed to look your best.

'Go keep him busy, then, while I wash up here,' Orla said, her mind racing. 'And get Maeve to bring over my best trousers, fresh underwear and the blouse I ironed yesterday in my wardrobe.'

She shoved her sister out of the stable entrance, then shot towards the washroom at the back of the stalls. Kicking off her boots, she ripped open the fly of her jeans. She could rinse herself here to get the stink off and then get changed before going to greet him.

Sophisticated and demure was out now, but she'd always been a tomboy and had never fitted into the racing high society her father frequented. She'd tried that by getting engaged to Patrick Quinn. And it had been a disaster.

What did you expect? Men have needs, Orla. And you're as frigid as a nun.

She flinched, remembering Patrick's parting words from five years back, and the sickening sight of him and Meghan O'Reilly wrapped around each other like superglue in the gazebo during their engagement party. Orla dumped her jeans by the sinks and ignored the shiver of humiliation that always accompanied the distressing memories.

Doesn't matter, you're well shot of him.

But Patrick had been right about one thing: she had never been any good at playing the flirtatious debutante. So trying to impress a playboy sheikh with her socialite credentials would always have been a stretch. Even if she'd had the time to prepare properly.

But if she changed into something not filthy, she could at least manage cool, calm and in control—something she needed to be to have any chance of persuading Karim Khan to let her stay at Calhouns.

The man knew their financial situation, that they were being forced to sell, so she didn't have much bargaining power.

She'd done a ton of Internet research on Khan last night, as soon as they'd got wind of Amari Corp's interest from the liquidator. From what she could tell their potential buyer was rich, entitled and arrogant, a royal prince who was used to having people like her at his beck and call and who was rich enough to think he could buy his way into a legacy that had taken her family ten generations to build. But she'd be damned if she'd let Crown Prince Whoever cut her out completely from the work she had dedicated her life to.

All she needed was a chance to prove to him she could still be useful at the stud. After all, she'd been as good as managing the place for five years now, ever since she turned seventeen and her father had become trapped in the well of grief left by her mother's death.

But she couldn't do that looking like Little Orphan Annie. From all the press reports she'd read, he was the sort of man who only paid attention to beautiful, sophisticated women with manicured nails, designer clothes and perfectly styled hair that reached down to their bums. The sort of woman she'd never been, even when she had fancied herself in love with the son of the neighbouring Quinn stud.

Standing in her camisole and panties, she grabbed the hose they used to wash the tack and turned it on. A whole body shiver raked her body as she doused her head with the frigid water. And cursed, loudly.

Why had Khan come five days early? Was he trying to catch her out?

A throat cleared loudly behind her.

'Ms Calhoun, I presume?' The deep, curt British accent had her swinging round so fast the hose flew out of her hand, sprinkling water everywhere.

Heat leapt into her cheeks and burned across her collarbone.

A tall man stood with his shoulder propped against the washroom door, his face cast into shadow by the sunshine, but she recognised him instantly from all the research.

What the ever-loving...?

She banded her arms across her chest to shield herself, but couldn't stop the humiliating shivers—as his cold assessing gaze set her freezing skin alight.

Seriously? Could she have made a worse impression? And how had he found her here so quickly?

Dervla, I'm going to strangle you.

'Mr... Mr Khan?' She stuck her chin out, trying to claw back a modicum of dignity, even though she knew she had to look like a drowned rat. 'We weren't expecting you until Friday. And what are you doing in the stables?'

He wore blue jeans, a black crew-neck sweater that clung to his impressively muscular chest, and black leather boots polished to a high gleam. His complexion was dark, his hair even darker. She had a sudden recollection of the villainous king in a book she'd read as a child who had been cruel and cold and all powerful, but also weirdly hot for the villain in a children's storybook. She'd loved that book once upon a time, reading it over and over again. And now she knew why.

'What am I doing here?' he said, the sarcastic tone cutting through her little reminiscence like a scalpel. 'I plan to buy your stud, Ms Calhoun. Today.'

Today?

Renewed panic sprinted up her spine, but then he turned into the light to grab the towel that hung from a peg on the washroom wall. And every thought flew out of her head bar one.

He's even hotter than the villainous king in Flinty O'Toole's Epic Quest.

Her lungs squeezed and the heat of mortification morphed into something a great deal more disturbing.

She already knew Karim Khan was stupidly handsome. She'd studied enough photographs of him last night at gala events, in tuxedos and designer suits, his hair perfectly styled as he paraded supermodels and actresses about as if they were accessories.

But the photos had not done him justice. In the flesh, and up close, and even without the luxury of a stylist, the man was quite simply breathtaking. Her heart literally stopped beating as she devoured the sight of firm, sensual lips, a strong jaw, high sculpted cheekbones and the long blade-like nose. The slight bump in the bridge and a sickle-shaped scar above his left eye marred the perfect symmetry of his face, but only made him look more rugged and masculine and overwhelming.

The burning heat in her cheeks shot through her veins, and her nipples, which were already like bullets, tightened into torpedoes. She squeezed her folded arms harder over her chest trying to quell the throbbing ache. She was more humiliated now than she'd been when she'd found her fiancé eating the face off another woman at her engagement party. And she'd always believed that humiliation could never be topped.

Wrong.

'Dry off,' he said, throwing her the towel.

She caught it one-handed, struggling to inflate her lungs when the light hit his face again and she saw the impatience in his eyes—which were a beautiful golden brown. Because, of course they were.

All the better to devastate you with, Orla. Because he's a god among men and you're a shivering, almost naked tomboy pauper.

As she frantically wrapped the towel around her nakedness, his gaze skimmed down, coasting over every inch of exposed skin until it got to the puddle of water forming at her bare feet.

'I'll meet you at the house in fifteen minutes,' he said, speaking to her as if she were a disobedient and particularly irritating ten-year-old. 'I need this deal finalised today.'

Despite her breathing difficulties, Orla felt her hackles rising.

Who did he think he was, speaking to her like that? Just because he was gorgeous and loaded and dry and fully clothed and she… Well… She wasn't.

But before she could come up with a suitably indignant reply, or gather enough courage—and breath—to actually enunciate it, the impossible man had strode back out of the stables and was gone.

CHAPTER TWO

'MR KHAN, I'M sorry to have kept you waiting. I hope Dervla offered you refreshments?'

Karim swung round from his lengthy contemplation of the impossibly green hills and hedgerows that surrounded the Calhoun stud to see the girl he had encountered twenty minutes ago in the stables crossing the faded rug towards him.

She had changed into a pair of simple black trousers and a white shirt, her damp red hair shoved back behind her ears. As she came into the light cast by the vast living room's bay windows, he realised she wore no make-up. He could still see the freckles sprinkled across her pale skin, which he had noticed earlier. She looked impossibly young and fresh-faced, even more so than she had dripping wet. He quashed the unbidden and unwanted spurt of heat at the memory of toned thighs, slender limbs and turgid nipples clearly visible through the wet fabric of her top.

He needed to find himself a new mistress if he was now responding to teenage tomboys.

'I don't have time for refreshments,' he said, leading with his impatience to disguise the inconvenient reaction that he knew had nothing to do with this fresh-faced, unsophisticated girl and everything to do with his recent sex drought. 'I have a proposal for purchasing the stud but to access it you need to agree to the sale today.'

The plan was a good one and foolproof and fairly straightforward. It hadn't taken him too long to figure out a better solution than dropping out of this deal—or the even more ludicrous solution Dane had outlined in Belgravia this morning—once he'd put his mind to it. He'd piloted the Puma himself to get here quickly and put the plan into action. Dane's prior warning was all he had needed to get ahead of his father.

He had also wanted to look over the property before he made his offer. But as soon as he'd walked into the stable yard he'd known. He wanted the Calhoun stud, whatever it took, because this was exactly what he had been looking for.

'I… I understand, Mr Khan, but I'm afraid I can't give you the agreement you seek.' Her eyes flickered with regret, even pain, but then she firmed her chin. 'The liquidators are handling the sale as this business is going under.'

He nodded. 'But you haven't yet, and you and your sister have inherited the business and the property, is this not correct?'

He'd already had his legal team double check the details while he was flying across the Irish Sea, so it was a rhetorical question, but she surprised him with the bluntness of her answer.

'Yes, we did, but we also inherited the debts. The property has already been remortgaged and we can't meet the interest payments any more.'

She and her sister would be left with less than nothing from the sale, by his calculation, because their father had frittered away the family business and more thanks to a gambling habit the family had kept secret for years.

'I understand you might want to get an even cheaper price by rushing the sale, but, believe me, you're already getting a bargain,' she said, the snap of pride in her voice suddenly making her seem older than her dewy skin and wide emerald eyes suggested.

'I'm not here to get a bargain, I'm here to offer you a chance to get out of this without debts still to pay.'

'How so?' she asked, the scepticism in her

face making him realise that, however young she was, she was not naïve.

'I will pay off all your debts today, by bank transfer, a sum which is in excess of what the business is worth, by approximately five million euro,' he said. 'Thus leaving you free to sell the property to me, immediately afterwards, for the sum of one euro, and the liquidators will still get their cut.'

It was a fair deal, a smart deal, for her as well as for him. She and her sister would be free and clear of her father's debts to start a new life. They would still be homeless but, as the daughter of one of racing's first families, she would no doubt have opportunities if she was willing to work hard, and much to his surprise—because he would have expected her to be an idle, entitled debutante instead of the girl he had found mucking out a stable—she seemed willing to do that much at least.

But more importantly, the property would not be put up for auction, so his father would have no opportunity to bid against him.

He saw her shock at his proposal.

'So, do we have a deal?' he said, confident of her answer. She had to know it was her only chance to get out from under the mountain of debt her father had left her with.

'No,' she said.

'I beg your pardon?' he snapped, surprised by the swell of something in his gut at her stubborn expression.

Why should he be impressed by her stupidity?

'I…' Heat blossomed in her cheeks. 'I… I said no. We don't have a deal. I have a request.'

He frowned. Was she actually serious?

'I don't think you understand, Ms Calhoun. This isn't a negotiation. It's a time-limited offer. And by far the best offer you are going to get. If I walk out that door today and I am not the new owner of Calhouns, the business will be sold at auction on Saturday as already arranged by the liquidators for a great deal less money than I am offering to spend on acquiring it today.'

'I understand that, but you need the deal signed today. Which gives me some leverage—won't you at least hear my request?'

She was trying to appear calm, but the riot of colour that had flared across her collarbone, and was giving him more unfortunate recollections of the sight of her barely clothed and soaking wet, suggested she was far from composed. His impatience downgraded a notch. The woman was an enigma in many ways… Who would have expected to find her mucking out her own stable, sweaty from work she could get an employee to do? Or cleaning herself down with a hose? But then again, from the state of her home—the faded carpets, worn furniture and peeling paintwork—he was getting the definite impression the Calhoun stud had been struggling financially for a lot longer than anyone had realised. How many staff did they even have? He'd only met an old man called Gerry who seemed to be manning the phones and an elderly housekeeper named Maeve so far.

'I'm listening,' he said, surprising himself with the decision to at least hear her out.

'I… I want a job.'

'What job?' he demanded, but strangely, the moment he said it, Dane's foolish suggestion from earlier that day echoed across his consciousness.

All you've gotta do is find yourself a woman who is greedy or desperate enough to be bought.

'Any job that will keep me at Calhouns. I've been managing the stud for the last five years. I know racing and horses, including everything there is to know about the ones we have left here.' She paused and he saw sadness and possibly even shame cross her face. 'My… My father stopped working with the horses after my mother died… So the successes we've had on the track in the last five years have been down to the team I've put together here. I'd really like the opportunity to keep working with them…'

She carried on talking, rushing through a list of her credentials and successes, which might or might not be true, but he was only listening with half an ear now as he turned over the possibility forming in his head.

He'd dismissed Dane's suggestion he take a wife in name only out of hand four hours ago. It was extreme and unnecessary and frankly ludicrous. But the benefits of keeping his father off his back—perhaps with an arrangement slightly less extreme—and having a Calhoun on his arm when entering the world of racing began to appeal to him as he watched her breasts rise and fall under the utilitarian shirt. Her eyes had widened with expectation as she continued to plead for a role at the stud.

He would need a lot more than simply her say-so to give her a position in management here, but he had another position that she could well be perfectly suited for. His reaction to her in the stables had been an anathema. She was the exact opposite of the sort of woman he would normally wish to have in his bed. Plain and unsophisticated, and far too slender... Although...

'How old are you?' he interrupted her frantic stream of information about herself.

'Umm, twenty-two.'

Relief coursed through him. So not a teenager. Thank God.

She might look fresh faced but from the awareness he had seen flash into her eyes when he had first discovered her in the stables, and the way her body had visibly responded to him, he suspected she was far from innocent. Even better.

'I'll consider giving you a job on my team here,' he said, deciding he could offer her that much, once he no longer had need of her. 'And throw in an extra million euro to keep your sister and yourself solvent after the sale goes through,' he added on the spur of the moment. It was only money after all and he wanted her compliant for what he had in mind. 'But I have a different position in mind for now.'

'That… That would be incredible,' she said, the blush turning her face to a becoming shade of pink. 'Whatever the position is I'm sure I can do it. I'm very adaptable. I realise you don't know me,' she said, getting ahead of herself again as he continued to study her. 'I'm happy to work a probation period, as long as I can keep working with our horses,' she added, a little frantically, the leap of desperate hope sparkling in her deep green eyes.

Desperate was good, eager to please even more so, it made her all but perfect for the role he had in mind. Except…

He let his gaze drift over her slender frame

again, the boyish clothes, the lack of make-up and the wild hair now beginning to curl around her ears, and still felt the inexplicable ripple of arousal that had surprised him in the stables, annoyingly.

But perhaps it was easily explained. She was pretty enough and her gauche, guileless demeanour made her quite different from the women he usually dated. Her novelty value would soon wear off, though, making this inexplicable reaction easy to control going forward. Not only that, but he planned to make finding a new mistress a top priority as soon as he returned to London. Once he had another woman in his bed, his attraction for this only passably pretty, artless tomboy would surely cease altogether.

'What job did you have in mind for me, Mr Khan?' she said, having finally wound down long enough to ask.

'I want you to become my fiancée, Ms Calhoun.'

CHAPTER THREE

'W-What did you say?' Orla croaked, the shock blasting up her torso with a humiliating surge of heat.

Had he just proposed to her? No, he couldn't have. She must be having some kind of weird auditory hallucination to go with her even weirder physical reaction to his sharp, dispassionate gaze—which she'd imagined a moment ago was assessing her as if she were one of the stud's prize brood mares.

'I said, I want you to become my fiancée.' The words left his lips and reached her eardrums, bringing with them another surge of inappropriate heat. But they still didn't make any sense whatsoever.

Perhaps she had lapsed into a coma? Or was this some bizarre pseudo-erotic dream? Maybe she hadn't woken up at all this morning, hadn't spent an hour on the gallops exercising Aderyn and another five hours mucking out the stalls?

Perhaps she was still in her bed upstairs, having fallen asleep scrolling through images of this man on the Internet…

'I… I…' she stuttered, wishing she could pinch herself to wake up. 'You want to marry me? But you don't even know me! We've never even dated.'

Or kissed, she thought irrationally, because that was all she could seem to focus on, along with his firm, sensual lips and that incredible face, which even with the inscrutable frown made him overwhelmingly gorgeous.

His eyebrows rose and then his mouth quirked in a wry smile. The once-over he gave her made every one of her pulse points pound, not to mention making the hot sweet spot between her thighs go molten—which had been overheating ever since she'd stood in front of him in the stables, soaking wet with torpedo nipples.

'I don't wish to marry you,' he said. 'Or date you,' he added as if she'd suggested something mildly amusing. She felt the bubble of anticipation she hadn't even realised was under her breastbone deflate and the renewed wash of humiliation roll over her. 'It would be an engagement in name only,' he continued. 'For which we would sign a binding contract. I would require you to be on my arm, and to act the dutiful, loving, soon-to-be wife, at any and all social and business events I frequent, to maintain the impression of a real relationship. We would have to establish that for the press—and for the racing fraternity, where I will use your connections to establish myself in the racing world…'

Connections? What connections?

She didn't have any connections in the racing world, because she'd always worked furiously behind the scenes, maintaining the fiction that the great Michael Calhoun was still the holder of the Calhoun legacy, long after he'd lost himself in his grief and his addiction. She had worked closely with the jockeys and the trainers and other stud managers, but she didn't know any of the big movers and shakers in the racing fraternity personally. Only the Quinns, the owners of the neighbouring stud, and after the devastating end of her engagement to Patrick they'd shunned her.

She'd been happy to remain anonymous, out of the way. Doing the work she loved with the horses. The socialite aspects of the racing world were something she had no interest in whatsoever and no aptitude for. Patrick had made that very clear to her.

She chewed on her bottom lip, knowing she couldn't tell Karim Khan the truth of the matter or he might withdraw his bizarre offer—which she was more than desperate enough to be seriously considering.

'But once everyone is convinced the engagement is real,' he continued, with about as much emotion as if he were discussing the weather, 'you will be free to carry on your own affairs, as long as they remain discreet.'

Affairs!

Her blush incinerated as she registered what he was saying. Somehow she managed to pluck a coherent question out of the fog of unwanted desire and utter confusion.

'How long would that be for?' she asked. 'That you'd need us to pretend to be in love?'

He stared at her, his jaw tightening at the mention of the L word, as if the reality of what he was asking her to fake hadn't occurred to him. But then it occurred to her, any man who would consider buying a fiancée probably didn't know the first thing about real relationships, let alone love.

'Until it is no longer useful for me to have a fiancée…' he said with supreme arrogance.

Right, of course, the parameters of this arrangement would be dictated by him, because he would be paying for the privilege.

'But, why would you be needing one?' she asked, curious now. If even the mention of love made him flinch, why would a man like him consider such an arrangement? Sure, maybe he wanted to be accepted in the racing world, but the truth was buying the stud would do that, he didn't need her. Even if she had the connections he thought she did. Money spoke louder than legacy in racing, just like any other sport. And surely he could have any woman he wanted on his arm? Why would he have to pay one to pretend to be in love with him? It was madness.

'A fake fiancée, that is?' she clarified, because the muscle in his jaw had only hardened.

'I'm paying you a million euros to do a job, Ms Calhoun, precisely because I have no desire to explain myself. Do you want it or not?'

She should tell him no. That she didn't want to be his fake fiancée. That she couldn't be bought. And that she would be terrible at it anyway. But somehow the words wouldn't come out of her mouth. Even though she now knew she definitely wasn't dreaming, this was actually real.

'Could Dervla and I keep the house? If we didn't take the money?' she asked. The old pile was the only home they'd ever known. And she didn't need a million euros, she just needed a chance.

He glanced around the room, probably taking in the ancient carpet, the few remaining pieces of furniture too old and worn to have any resale value, the damp patch in the corner by the dresser and the faded spots on the wallpaper where art had once been hung but had long since been sold—to pay for her father's gambling debts.

Michael Calhoun had needed an escape from the pain of losing the love of his life, her mother. Unfortunately his escape had eventually drained any semblance of the man she had once known, until all that was left was a shadow. The house reflected that.

'You can keep the property instead if you wish as I have no need of it. But I will require you to be at my beck and call, and to travel with me for the events I mentioned.'

Her chest tightened, the sinking sensation in her stomach not making a lot of sense. This was a business deal effectively. She couldn't allow her emotions to get in the way. He didn't want *her*, he wanted her name, her heritage and, for reasons unknown, he needed a fiancée.

This was a chance, she told herself, to keep her family home, and to give her sister a place to live while she was at Trinity. Because Dervla could easily commute into Dublin from here. Of course, if Khan found out Orla was socially dyslexic and knew nothing about how to impress racing high society or any other high society, and that she was also a virgin, he might withdraw the offer. How was she supposed to behave like a woman in love when she'd never even taken a lover, and certainly not a man as— she drew in a deep breath—as far out of her league as him?

But even as all the things that could go wrong bombarded her, the hot ache between her thighs refused to go away.

'When would you need me to start?' she asked.

A rueful smile tilted his lips and his gaze sharpened. 'You would return with me to London tonight and we will sign the engagement contract first thing in the morning.'

So soon. Her mind began to race again, along with her pulse rate, the hot spot in her abdomen dropping deeper into her sex.

'I am attending the Jockeys' Ball at The Chesterton Hotel tomorrow evening,' he continued. 'We can announce our engagement and the sale of the stud at the same time.'

She blinked and swallowed around the wodge of panic working its way up her throat and threatening to gag her.

Of course, The Jockeys' Ball was tomorrow at the luxury six-star hotel in Soho. Everyone who was anyone in racing would be there, as it was the main social event to mark the middle of the racing calendar in Europe. She'd attended only once, with Patrick and her father, five years ago, and hated every minute of it. Feeling exposed and inadequate and out of her depth. How much more out of her depth would she be if she were there posing as Karim Khan's trophy fiancée? But even as the panic began to consume her, she forced herself to breathe. Once they had signed the contract, he wouldn't be able to change his mind. Would he?

She'd just have to wing it. And hope to heck he didn't find out how inadequate she was for the role he wanted her to play before tomorrow night—when it would become all too apparent.

'So, do we have a deal, Ms Calhoun?' he demanded. The tone was arrogant and commanding, those golden-brown eyes still doing diabolical things to her heart rate. She needed to get that reaction under control, asap. 'What is your first name, by the way?' he asked.

The question was so incongruous, she almost laughed. He'd just asked her to pretend to be madly in love with him, and he didn't even know her given name?

'It's Orla,' she said, feeling as if she were mounting a large, unbroken stallion for the first time—both terrified and yet also weirdly exhilarated.

She and Dervla would have their home, and she could continue to work with the horses.

Eventually. All she had to do was cling on for the ride in the next few weeks and months—because surely he wouldn't want her for much longer than that—and hope to heck she didn't end up breaking her neck, metaphorically speaking.

'So, Orla, what's it to be?' he pushed, making no effort to hide his impatience.

'Yes,' she said, with a firmness and determination she didn't feel. 'Yes, we do have a deal, Mr Khan.'

'Call me Karim,' he said, although it sounded like an order rather than a request. He tugged his smartphone out of his pocket and she realised she had already been dismissed. 'You have half an hour to pack—don't forget your passport,' he said as he checked something on his phone. 'We can do all the necessary paperwork on the sale and the engagement contract after we get to London.' His gaze locked back on her face. 'I wish to take another look round the stud, so I'll meet you at the Puma at a quarter to two,' he said. 'Don't leave me waiting this time.'

Moments later, his footsteps had faded down the hallway.

Orla stood in the empty room and wrapped her arms round her midriff to hold in the shudder of panic and something a great deal more volatile. She walked to the window and gazed out on the land that had always been her home. The only place where she felt grounded and whole and significant.

What she'd just agreed to do was madness. The arrogant, entitled, overwhelming man had even refused to tell her why he needed a fake fiancée. And why on earth he might have picked her for such a role.

Karim Khan, Crown Prince of Zafar, held all the power in this situation and she none.

But beggars could not be choosers, and she refused to regret taking his devil's bargain— Dervla and the horses and their home were worth it.

To have a future free of debt, and the opportunity to continue living in the place she'd thought they'd lost, was something she couldn't even have dreamed of when she'd woken up this morning before dawn. Life had been so hard ever since her father passed in a car accident a year ago—much longer than that, truth be told, ever since her mother's tragic death while riding on the gallops five years ago had effectively robbed her and Dervla of their father too.

She and her sister deserved this chance.

All she had to do now was find a way to show everyone she had what it took to make a crown prince fall hopelessly in love with her—when she knew full well she didn't. Not even close.

This will be an adventure, she told herself staunchly.

But then the bottom dropped out of her stomach and heat careered through her veins as she spied the tall, indomitable, commanding man she had just agreed to attach herself to for the foreseeable future walk out of the house and take long strides across the lawn towards the stables.

She hadn't even managed to convince Patrick she would make him a good wife, and now she was going to have to pretend to be engaged to a man who could give her breathing difficulties and inappropriate goosebumps just by looking at her. A man she knew virtually nothing about. And what she did know only made him a hundred times more intimidating.

Orla Calhoun, what in the name of all that is holy have you gone and done now?

CHAPTER FOUR

'MISS CALHOUN, YOU must wake up now. Mr Khan wishes to see you downstairs.'

Orla blinked furiously, waking from a particularly vivid dream, to find an older woman smiling at her. She jerked upright, taking in the feel of expensive cotton sheets and the bright sunlight streaming through the large multi-paned window opposite and shining onto a suite of luxury furniture.

'Hi,' she said, as the reality of where she was and what she had agreed to yesterday spun back through her groggy brain.

Standing in the stables, dripping wet, her nipples so hard they ached as Karim Khan's golden gaze awakened every one of her nerve-endings. His overpowering presence in her faded parlour, asking, no, *demanding* she become his fiancée. The mad scramble to ensure Dervla would look after the horses to her satisfaction before Khan's team arrived. The helicopter ride across the Irish Sea and the British countryside, before they'd flown over the nightlights of London to land on the rooftop heliport of Khan's mansion in Belgravia.

He'd hardly spoken to her since she had agreed to become his fake fiancée, spending the time while piloting the chopper talking to a series of subordinates through his headphones. Once they'd arrived, she'd been ushered into the house and served dinner alone in the suite of rooms she now occupied, and then she'd dropped into bed…

'Is it Mrs Williams?' she asked, trying to remember the woman's name from the night before. She was one of Mr Khan's staff. His housekeeper, Orla was fairly sure, but everything about the evening before had been a blur, the extravagant luxury of Khan's home and the thought of what she'd agreed to do making it hard for Orla to concentrate when she'd been introduced to about twenty people before being brought to her own luxury suite.

She'd dreamt of him, she realised, during the night. That intense gaze had woken her frequently causing the hot weight in her sex, and the tight ache in her breasts.

'Call me Edith, dear,' the woman said as she laid a breakfast tray on a table by the window with practised efficiency. 'Mr Khan has employed a stylist to acquire a new wardrobe for you. But I had your clothes from last night washed and pressed for the meeting this morning.' The housekeeper smiled. 'I hope that's okay, but I couldn't find anything else in your luggage that looked suitable when I unpacked it.'

'That's perfect,' Orla said, remembering the one humiliating conversation she'd had with Khan before boarding the helicopter in Kildare.

'Do you have any suitable clothing with you?' he'd asked, casting a cursory glance at the rucksack she'd packed hastily in the half-hour he'd given her.

'You didn't give me much time to pack,' she'd replied, not wanting to admit she had nothing suitable for the sort of rarefied social gatherings he was probably expecting her to attend. She hadn't had money for new clothes in years. Plus she lived in boots and jeans and T-shirts to work with the horses, and was already wearing her best clothing.

He'd nodded and lifted the rucksack into the helicopter. End of conversation. Obviously he had made a note of her lack of a decent wardrobe and arranged for new clothing.

She tried not to feel even more humiliated—at the thought of having to be dressed by him—as she climbed out of the bed and tugged on the silk robe that Edith had laid out at the end of the bed.

'The solicitor has already arrived to finalise the sale,' the housekeeper said. 'Mr Khan is keen to see you as soon as possible downstairs.' The woman sent Orla a warm, uncomplicated smile. 'He's even more impatient than usual. You two must be very much in love.'

Say what, now?

'Um, yes,' Orla murmured, struggling to control the full body blush that was currently incinerating her.

So the Crown Prince hadn't told his staff the truth about their engagement.

'Please call me Orla, by the way,' she added, unused to the formality with her own family's staff. The few she had been able to retain had become friends and allies over the last few years.

'Oh, I couldn't do that, Miss Calhoun. Mr Khan wouldn't approve,' the housekeeper replied. 'After all, you are going to become the Crown Princess of Zafar.'

The surreal unreality of the situation struck Orla again as she watched the housekeeper finish laying out the breakfast.

'Now, I must get back downstairs. Would you like me to send up one of the maids, to help you dress?' she asked.

'No, really, I'm good,' Orla replied.

'Can I tell the Crown Prince you'll be down in half an hour?' Edith asked, the hopeful look making Orla wonder if the housekeeper was going to get chastised by her employer if she didn't get a move on.

'Yes, absolutely,' Orla said, even though the last thing she wanted to do was see him again. There wasn't much point in postponing the meeting, though, especially if it was going to get Edith into trouble.

The woman smiled then left Orla standing alone in the room.

Abandoning the breakfast, she headed for the suite's palatial bathroom. With her stomach churning she wouldn't be able to swallow a bite of the lavish display of fresh fruit, pastries, pancakes and eggs and bacon, laid out on the table.

Her stomach turned over again. And even if she could, she doubted she would be able to keep it down once she got downstairs.

Twenty-nine minutes later, Orla arrived downstairs, to be greeted by a butler who led her to Khan's study, a large, beautifully appointed room that looked onto the mansion's extensive gardens.

Her heart pummelled her tonsils as she spotted Khan's muscular frame silhouetted against the large mullioned window. In dark grey expertly tailored suit trousers and a white shirt rolled up at the sleeve, showing off the dark skin of his forearms, he looked like exactly what he was—a rich, powerful and supremely confident playboy prince. He turned as she entered the room. And her lungs squeezed.

Correction: a rich, powerful, supremely confident and impossibly hot playboy prince.

'Orla, at last,' he said. The familiarity of her name on his lips made her pulse rate accelerate as he strode across the thick carpeting to greet her. But when he took her hand and lifted her fingers, she jolted, the hot weight in her abdomen ready to detonate, as he skimmed her knuckles with his lips.

It was the first time he had touched her, let alone with such familiarity—the feel of his lips, firm and entitled, had sensation racing through her body. She struggled to relax as his eyes narrowed with displeasure.

Then she spotted the other man in the room for the first time.

The charade had begun, she realised, and she had already made a mess of things.

Was he angry with her? He had to be—he was paying her a great deal of money to play his besotted bride-to-be. But the slight frown had gone and all she could see in his gaze was something that looked like scepticism.

Taking her hand in a firm grip, he folded her arm over his, trapping her against his side to escort her across the room. Unwanted desire raced over her skin, but she forced herself to breathe.

Act natural, you're supposed to be lovers, you dope.

'This is the head of my legal team, Orla, Phillip Carstairs, who has some papers for you to sign,' he said, introducing her to the other man.

'Ms Calhoun.' The dignified man in his fifties greeted her with a warm smile. 'I'm so pleased to meet you at last. Karim has been telling me all about your whirlwind courtship. My wife will be starry-eyed when I give her the details,' the solicitor added, without a hint of sarcasm, as he held out his hand.

'Thank you, Mr Carstairs.' She shook his hand, trying to stop her own from shaking and look suitably excited—while wondering what the story was Khan had told his solicitor. It might have been nice if he'd bothered to clue her in.

'Yes, it all happened so very fast,' she added, directing an awestruck look at the man beside her.

Not surprisingly, that wasn't at all hard to fake, as she felt Khan's biceps flex and the warm skin of his bare forearm—lightly furred with hair—burned her fingertips.

Khan turned his searing gaze on her.

'Would you like Phillip to take you through the sales contract for the stud before you sign, Orla?' he asked. It seemed to be a genuine offer, even though she could sense his impatience.

'Does it contain everything we agreed?' she asked.

'Of course,' he said.

She nodded as Carstairs laid out the papers. 'I'm happy to sign it now,' she said, having skimmed through the details. Oddly she trusted him. The perfunctory nature of their relationship so far made it very clear he viewed her as nothing more than another of his employees. Bought and paid for. He hadn't quibbled about any of her requirements and had actually been much more generous than he needed to be. Money was clearly no object for him. She needed to view this situation as a job. And nothing more. A job she wanted to do well—she couldn't risk him changing his mind.

She could see she had pleased him when the wrinkle that had formed on his forehead when she reacted so violently to a simple hand buzz disappeared.

'Excellent,' he said.

'We'll have the contract couriered to your sister in Kildare to sign too. I understand she has already agreed to these terms as well?' Carstairs said as he handed her a gold pen.

'Yes, that's correct,' Orla said, recalling Dervla's joy at the news they would be able to stay in their home with no debts to pay.

Orla signed her name in bold fluid strokes. The nuns who had schooled her would be proud, she thought, grateful that her fingers had finally stopped shaking.

It wasn't nearly as hard as she had assumed to sign away her heritage. The stud was just a business. It was the horses she loved, and her sister, and their home. The chance to get out of the shadow of debt that had been hanging over her for so long felt strangely liberating.

But then Carstairs laid out some more papers in both English and what looked like Arabic. 'Would you like to read through these, Ms Calhoun?' the solicitor asked. 'This is the English translation of the traditional Zafari Engagement Contract. I'm afraid it's a legal requirement in Mr Khan's country of origin that the Crown Prince's engagement must be accompanied by a binding contract, to ensure the cultural traditions as well as the economic interests of Zafar are observed and protected before the couple enter into a marriage.'

Orla nodded, then skimmed through the pages—

the small type blurring before her eyes. She didn't need to read them, because they weren't ever going to get actually married. 'Great,' she said at last.

Khan's hand rested on the small of her back, rubbing absently as he signed the original first. He handed her the pen, still warm from his fingers, and Carstairs pointed out the places where she needed to sign and initial the paperwork. She could feel Khan's gaze focussed on her, the hand on her back like a heavy controlling weight. She doubted he was even aware of what he was doing, the caress as nonchalant as it was impersonal. But the sensation sprinting up her spine from his touch was anything but.

Her penmanship was forgotten this time as she dashed off each signature and initial as quickly as possible. She needed to get this over, before she lost her nerve—or, worse, reacted in a way that would give away, not just her lack of familiarity with Khan and their so-called whirlwind courtship, but also her complete lack of sophistication when it came to being touched with such easy familiarity by a man.

She'd shared kisses with Patrick, of course, when they'd been engaged. But she'd been a girl then—naïve and eager, sheltered and completely untried. And Patrick, although having a great deal more sexual experience than she had at the time, had been a boy, not a man like

Khan, who could light bonfires across her back with a simple caress.

At last all the paperwork was done.

But then she heard Mr Carstairs laugh and murmur, 'Perhaps you should kiss your new fiancée, Karim.'

'Yes,' the deep voice said beside her.

She tried to control her trembling, scared he might be able to feel it, as he turned her in his arms and rested his hands on her hips. He was studying her, the curiosity in his gaze both pragmatic and yet somehow exhilarating.

Could he see how inexperienced she was, and how much his nearness affected her? She hoped not, terrified he might annul the engagement before it had even begun.

He lifted his hand and placed it on her neck, holding her gently in place. The calluses on his palm, calluses she would not have expected, rasped across the sensitive skin, making her brutally aware of the light pressure. His thumb rubbed casually across the well in her collarbone, back and forth, as he watched her—the golden shards in the brown of his irises so vivid they mesmerised her. He lowered his head, gradually, allowing her to taste the toothpaste on his breath as it whispered across her lips. His thumb paused, and pressed into her collarbone, trapping the frantic butterfly flutters of her pulse.

She suddenly had the vision of one of Calhouns' stable hands stroking their highly strung mare, Cliona, to quiet her for Aderyn to mount her. The thought turned the tremble into a violent shiver.

She stiffened. He had to have felt that now.

His other hand tightened on her hip, gentle, yet controlling, and even more overwhelming as he whispered for only her to hear, 'Shh, Orla. Breathe.'

Then his lips finally settled on hers, firm, seeking, confident, commanding.

Electricity seemed to arch through her body, the yearning so swift and so strong, she forgot everything but the scent, the taste, the touch of his lips. The solid wall of his chest pressed against her aching breasts as he dragged her closer.

Her hands flattened against his waist, grasping his linen shirt in greedy fists, and holding on for dear life as the storm of sensation battered her body, while her heart thumped her ribcage and sank deep into her abdomen, throbbing painfully between her thighs.

His tongue slid across her mouth demanding entry and she opened instinctively. His guttural groan of conquest matched her sob of surrender as she melted against him, her body softening and swelling in its most intimate places as his tongue swept in.

He explored in demanding delicious strokes, and she made tentative licks back, the yearning so intense now, the longing so real and over-powering she knew that whatever it was she wanted from him, she needed it now.

He tore his lips free, and stared down at her. His hands lifted to cradle her cheeks, and tilt her face up. She saw surprise flicker in his dark eyes as he studied her, but knew it was nothing compared with the shock careering through her body. Her breathing was so ragged her lungs felt trapped in her ribcage.

The loud throat-clearing from beside them had them both swinging round.

'Congratulations, you two,' Phillip Carstairs said with an avuncular smile on his face. 'I would suggest you start planning the wedding as soon as possible.'

The heat that still pounded between Orla's thighs and burned on her lips exploded into her cheeks like a mushroom cloud.

Khan let go of her face at last as he turned to his solicitor. 'Thanks, Phil, now perhaps you'd like to get lost, so my new fiancée and I can have some privacy.'

Carstairs gathered up the papers Orla had just

signed, then sent them both a mocking bow. 'I'd say enjoy your engagement, Karim,' he said. 'But I can see there is really no need.' He held the papers up. 'I'll send the engagement contract through to the Zafari Ruling Council so they can inform your father of the good news.'

Orla felt Karim tense beside her, before Carstairs bid them both goodbye and left the room.

The door closed behind him.

'I should go too,' Orla murmured, brutally aware of the embarrassment scalding her cheeks and the heavy weight that had swollen to impossible proportions in her sex. Luckily Khan seemed a million miles away, his expression both strained and annoyed.

She had no idea what had caused his displeasure. But before she could make a quick getaway he snagged her wrist.

'Not so fast,' he said, drawing her to a halt. 'That kiss was unexpected.'

'I… I was just trying to be convincing,' she said, not even convincing herself with the desperate lie.

She could see she hadn't convinced him either, when his brows drew together, the puzzled expression doing nothing to cool the passionate intensity in the golden brown of his irises.

'You did an extremely thorough job,' he said,

the mocking tone making it very clear he knew her response had been entirely genuine.

She tried to look away to hide the mortification running riot on her cheeks now, but he tucked a knuckle under her chin and forced her gaze back to his.

'Just tell me one thing—are you a virgin?' he demanded.

Her eyes widened. How had he guessed?

'Because if you are,' he continued, the dark frown on his face accusing her, 'we'll have to call this off.'

'I'm not a virgin,' she lied, finally managing to gather her wits enough to shake her head. 'I've had several lovers,' she added. 'Lots of lovers. I was... I was engaged five years ago,' she continued, desperately trying to dispel the scepticism lurking in his eyes. She couldn't lose this deal—the chance to stay at Calhouns, to secure a future free of debt, to continue to work with the horses she loved. But somehow those reasons seemed shallow and insignificant as the desire continued to spark and sizzle.

'Do you really think I would have kissed you like that if I was?' she finished.

Once upon a time, she'd been a terrible liar, but she'd had considerable practice in the last five years, convincing everyone from jockeys to trainers to racing managers that Calhouns wasn't struggling to stay afloat. She drew on every last ounce of that experience now to convince him.

He continued to study her, the desire he was making no attempt to hide both disturbing and yet at the same time terrifyingly exciting.

'No, I suppose not,' he said finally.

He shook his head slightly, as if trying to jog something loose, then let go of her wrist abruptly.

Shoving his hands into the pockets of his suit trousers, he continued to stare at her, the penetrating gaze both intrusive and disturbingly intimate.

She folded her arms over her midriff, feeling exposed and desperately wary, far too aware of the stinging on her lips where their kiss had got so far out of control.

But she forced herself not to relinquish eye contact. If she was going to persuade him she wasn't a virgin, she needed to be bold now, even if her hormones were still rampaging through her body like toddlers on a sugar rush... And she'd never felt more insecure or unstable in her entire life.

She didn't know what the heck had happened to her. Maybe she didn't have very much experience, but she'd never responded like that to any of Patrick's kisses.

How had she forgotten so easily who he was, and that this 'engagement' was a charade? The minute his lips had claimed hers, even before that, the minute he had looked at her with that intense focus back at the stable yard, it was as if her body were no longer her own. That it belonged to him, and he could command it and destroy it at will.

She couldn't let that happen again, or she would lose. Not just this deal, but also her sense of self.

This engagement was a means to an end for him. A means to an end he hadn't even bothered to confide in her. She was bought and paid for, a fiancée in name only, until he no longer required her services, then she would be discarded.

He tugged his fingers through his hair, sending the expertly styled waves into disarray, still staring at her as if he were trying to decipher a particularly thorny problem.

At last he nodded. 'I'll see you tonight at seven,' he said.

Her breath gushed out as she realised she'd got away with her lie. For now anyhow.

'We'll go through the story I've made up to explain our relationship en route to the ball,' he added. 'So you don't trip up again.'

It was a reprimand. But she didn't care as

she nodded and left, just so relieved to be out of the room.

As she raced up the stairs back to her suite, though, she wasn't sure any more if she was more concerned about Khan cancelling their contract, and leaving her sister and herself destitute, or her inexplicable and uncontrollable reaction to a simple kiss.

CHAPTER FIVE

'YOUR HIGHNESS, YOUR fiancée is waiting for you in the vestibule.'

Karim glanced up from his phone to find Muhammed, his butler, standing in the doorway to his study.

Your fiancée.

The words reverberated in his skull… and, unfortunately, his groin, reminding him of their kiss that morning. A kiss that was supposed to have been as false as everything else about this arrangement, and had been anything but. Orla Calhoun's artless eager reaction had been unexpected, but much more unexpected had been his own response. The fresh sweet taste of her lips, the sound of her stunned sob, the feel of her taut, trembling body softening against his, and her fingers gripping his shirt as if she were in a high wind and he were her only anchor. The combination had set fire to the heat already smouldering in his groin, ever since the day before.

All of which was a problem.

He had picked this woman precisely because he had expected his desire to die. Clearly that had been an error, because after that one taste of her he had not been able to forget the effect she'd had on him. Or the fact he wanted more of her. Desiring her could cause complications he did not need.

Thank God, at least she wasn't inexperienced, as he had at first suspected. Ever since their kiss he had been considering the problem, and decided that perhaps they could change the terms of their contract. However he needed to be absolutely sure this attraction was not going to get any more out of control. Already he did not appreciate the fact his reaction had been almost as uncontrolled as hers.

'Tell her I'll be with her in a moment,' he said, tucking the phone back into the breast pocket of his tuxedo.

Tonight's event would be long and tedious. Her racing connections would come in handy to smooth his passage into this world. It would also present a good chance to gauge exactly how volatile his reaction was to this woman.

'Yes, Your Highness,' the butler said, but then his usually formal expression softened. 'And can I congratulate you again on your engagement?' he added, his craggy face flushing.

'Your fiancée is indeed exquisite and so charming. I had no idea Michael Calhoun's daughter was such a beauty. No wonder he hid her away.'

What?

Karim frowned as his usually close-mouthed and now clearly besotted butler bowed and left. Orla, whatever the strange spell she seemed to have cast over him, could hardly be described as a great beauty. Could she? And what did Muhammed mean by Calhoun hiding her away? Karim had never attended any racing events, waiting for the right opportunity to buy into a pastime that had captivated him as a boy but which he'd had no time to indulge properly until now. Perhaps he should have done more homework before suggesting this association? The truth was it wasn't at all like him to make business decisions on the spur of the moment. That said, he always went with his gut instinct when opportunity arose, and Orla's circumstances had seemed perfect for what he had in mind.

He rebuttoned his tuxedo jacket and spotted, on the edge of his desk, the velvet ring box that had been delivered earlier in the day. He scooped up the box and stared at it. He'd had the engagement ring selected by the stylist. He shoved it into his trouser pocket without opening it, annoyed by the moment of hesitation. It hardly mattered what the ring looked like, as long as it fitted.

He marched out of his study, down the hallway towards the front entrance and then stopped dead as he spotted the woman standing with her back to him. The silver backless gown shimmered in the light from the chandelier, the iridescent material draping over her slender curves like water. The vibrant red waves of her hair had been pinned up with a series of diamonds, which glittered like stars in a sunset. The chignon should have looked supremely elegant… But somehow, the tendrils falling down against her nape made him think of the wild, untamed way she had returned his kiss.

Karim's breath backed up in his lungs, the shot of arousal so sudden it made him tense. He planted his hands in his pockets, the urge to slip the delicate straps off her shoulders and place his mouth on the smooth arch of her neck so strong he had to take a moment.

'Orla,' he murmured, and she spun round.

What the…?

Shock ricocheted through his system, swiftly followed by a need so sharp he couldn't contain it, let alone control it.

'What the hell are you wearing?' he growled before he could stop himself as the shot of desire detonated in his groin.

His gaze devoured her high breasts, the neckline of the gown giving him a glimpse of her cleavage, which was as torturous as it was tantalising. She was not wearing a bra.

'You don't… You don't like it?' she asked as she crossed her arms over her waist, as if trying to shield herself from his view.

His gaze jerked away from her breasts to see the flush of embarrassment on her face. Smoky make-up had been deftly applied around her eyes and her full lips given a coating of something glossy, which only made the yearning to taste them again all the more compelling.

But beneath that, he could see the devastating combination of embarrassment and awareness in her expression.

He forced himself to move across the foyer, attempting to dial down his overreaction each step of the way. He'd seen other women wearing far less at the sort of society functions he attended. Hell, women he'd actually been dating had worn gowns that were a great deal more revealing, and he'd never had a problem with it.

Was this something to do with the fact she was his fiancée? But that was insane—this wasn't a real engagement. And even if it were, since when had he ever been possessive about a woman?

In truth there was nothing wrong with the

dress, he tried to tell himself, as his gaze lingered again on the shimmering material. No doubt it was the height of fashion, probably made by some much-sought-after designer who charged a fortune to display his new fiancée's lush, coltish physique for everyone to see. In fact, it did exactly what he had asked the stylist to do: made the most of Orla's assets. Unfortunately, he had not realised when he requested such an approach quite how many assets she had, or how much he would not want to allow everyone else to enjoy them.

'It's okay, Orla, the dress is good,' he managed past the lump of lust forming in his throat.

Far too damn good.

He touched her elbow, her instinctive shudder of awareness reminiscent of the livewire moment he'd touched her for the first time that morning.

As she turned into the light, he became momentarily transfixed by the sprinkle of freckles across her cleavage and the glimpse of her naked breast visible at the edge of the gown. Her pulse pounded visibly against the hollow in her neck, giving him a lungful of her scent. The intoxicating aroma reminded him of a country garden, the subtle perfume of wild flowers and the earthy scent of freshly mown grass. He bit down on the urge to nuzzle the translucent skin and nibble kisses along the delectable line of her collarbone.

'Are you sure the dress is okay, Mr Khan?' she said, forcing him back to the present. 'The stylist might have another if you don't like it…' Small white teeth tugged on her bottom lip.

Was she really as sexually experienced as she claimed? he wondered, not for the first time. And why the hell did her guilelessness only intoxicate him more?

'I like it,' he said, which had to be the understatement of the millennium. 'You don't have time to change. And stop calling me Mr Khan. My name is Karim, Orla. Use it.'

Cupping her elbow, he led her out of the door to their waiting car. He needed to get this night over with, so he could think. He wasn't making any more rash decisions where this woman was concerned.

When was the last time a woman had affected him to this extent? The truth was his affairs had become jaded and dull in recent years, and while this livewire attraction was inconvenient, even unwanted, it also had the potential to be pleasurable for both of them.

But before he renegotiated the terms of their liaison, he needed to be sure his new fiancée wasn't going to spring any more unwanted surprises on him.

He held open the passenger door of the convertible he'd selected to drive to the venue tonight. As Orla climbed into the low-slung car, he noticed the split in the gown's skirt, revealing a generous glimpse of pale, toned thigh.

He cursed inwardly as the wave of heat shot straight back into his groin.

He slammed the door and walked around to the driver's side. First thing tomorrow, he was firing the damn stylist.

Mr Khan... Karim was angry with her, and she didn't know what she'd done wrong.

She'd done everything he'd asked. The dress had made her feel exposed and foolish—she'd never worn anything so skimpy before, or so beautiful. But the stylist had insisted it was perfect for her figure and would turn her new fiancé into her 'slave'—the stylist's words, not hers. Of course, the stylist—like the rest of Karim's employees—didn't know this wasn't a real engagement... And that even if she danced naked in front of him it wouldn't turn him into her slave.

But the minute she'd heard the gruff whisper behind her, and turned to see Karim standing staring at her in the vestibule, that intense gaze making her skin prickle and pulse beneath the sheer fabric of the glittery gown, she'd known something was terribly wrong. Because he didn't look pleased, he looked… Volatile.

His movements and his demeanour had been stiff and formal ever since, as if he were trying to hold onto his temper. The shock of seeing him in a tuxedo, his dark good looks somehow even more compelling and dangerous in the formal wear, hadn't helped.

She sat in the car, trying to gather her thoughts and figure out what she could do to make things better between them. If only she had more experience of intimate relationships she might have more of a clue.

He climbed into the car beside her, slammed the door, then pressed a button on the expensive car's state-of-the-art dashboard.

As the engine purred, he reached into his trouser pocket and produced a velvet box.

'Put this on,' he said, as he handed her the box.

She opened the small container. Her breathing slowed, the well-oiled vibrations of the powerful car amplifying the thundering in her ears.

Nestled in the box's black satin lining was an exquisite ring of interwoven rose-gold and silver bands, studded with diamonds but crowned by an emerald. The misty green of the gem reminded her of the colour of the fields in Kildare when the sun hit them for the first time on a summer morning.

'It's stunning,' she managed, round the strange swelling in her throat, as it occurred to her how different this moment was from the day Patrick Quinn had given her an engagement ring. Back then, of course, she'd believed Pat loved her, because she'd been a child with foolish romantic notions, instead of a woman with debts she couldn't repay.

Her heart hurt as the impact of what she'd done that morning—become engaged to a man for money—hit her solidly in the solar plexus.

She touched the ring, but her fingers were trembling too violently for her to pull it out of the box.

'Here,' he said, as he took the box from her. He plucked the engagement band out. 'Give me your hand.'

She placed her left hand in his, far too aware of the warmth of his palm as his fingers closed over hers, gently, in a silent gesture to stop the trembling. Remarkably it worked, his touch so compelling it seemed to command her obedience.

'Which finger does it go on?' he asked.

Her gaze lifted to his, to find him watching her, but instead of frustration or fury what she saw was contemplation, and something else, something that still looked remarkably volatile but not necessarily aimed at her.

'The ring finger,' she said. But when he went to thread the ring on, her finger wobbled.

'Is something wrong?' he asked.

His golden gaze was still fixed on her face. The warmth in her cheeks ignited, but she forced herself to remain pragmatic, even if the aching in her chest had got so much worse as a thought spun into her brain unbidden. What would it be like to have a man as passionate and powerful as Karim Khan truly care for you? To want to cherish and protect you?

'No, nothing,' she said hastily, dismissing the weak, pointless yearning as best she could. She didn't want to have this situation be real. She didn't need any man to cherish and protect her, and certainly not a man like Karim Khan. He might be rich and powerful, but he was also taciturn and cynical and cold... And far too overwhelming for the likes of her. Falling for a man like him would be even more fraught with danger than falling for a man like her skank of an ex-fiancé.

She squeezed her fingers into a fist then straightened them again to stop the trembling. She didn't want him to think she was some kind of foolish romantic, or, worse, that she had any kind of misconceptions about what this relationship was.

He stroked the ring finger with his thumb, then slipped the band on, pushing it down. His thumb slid back over the knuckle, then he let go of her hand. She missed the warmth of his touch instantly.

Her pulse began to punch her collarbone.

'Thank goodness it fits,' he said, his voice a husky murmur.

The tiny diamonds sparkled in the light from an overhead street lamp, exquisite and yet ethereal. She curled her fingers back into a fist and placed both her hands in her lap, painfully aware of the buzz of sensation his touch had ignited, and the cold weight of the ring that didn't really belong to her.

The engagement ring must have cost an absolute fortune, the insignia on the box from London's most exclusive jewellers. Perhaps it was the thought of possessing something so valuable, even for a little while, that was the problem, not the significance of having Karim Khan place his ring on her finger, when that had no real significance at all.

'I'll be sure to take good care of it for you,' she said. 'Until you need it back.'

'Why would I need it back?' he asked, the

cutting edge back. Had she done something else wrong?

She stared at his face, the strong planes and angles even more striking cast into shadow by the street lamp. Was he serious? 'Won't you need it when you get engaged for real? It must have cost a fortune.'

He let out a harsh chuckle, as if she'd said something particularly stupid. 'Keep it. The stylist picked it out for you, so it's unlikely to suit any other woman.' He shifted the car into gear. 'And once this is over, I certainly don't intend to do it again.'

As the car peeled away from the kerb, the critical comment ripped through her show of confidence, to the neglected girl beneath.

The light summer breeze whipped at her skin. She squeezed her fist, determined to ignore the ring, and the lump of inadequacy forming in her throat.

This isn't about you, it's not personal. The engagement is a means to an end, he's made no secret of that.

But unfortunately, despite her frantic pep talk, there didn't seem to be much she could do about the heavy weight of his disapproval sinking into the pit of her stomach.

Getting through the next few hours pretending to belong in Karim Khan's rarefied world—

and present the picture of a loving fiancée, when she knew she was no kind of fiancée—suddenly seemed insurmountable.

'I told Phillip Carstairs and my financial advisors we met when I visited the stud, and that my decision to pay off the estate's debts were a result of my affection for you.'

'I'm sorry, what?' she said, too preoccupied with her own evolving misery to take stock of what he'd said.

'The story of our whirlwind romance,' he clarified. 'I left it vague, but if anyone questions you simply say the engagement is based on our shared love of horse racing and our…' he paused '…our considerable chemistry.' He glanced her way, trapping her in that intense gaze for a second before he returned his attention to the road. Even so it was enough to reignite the familiar bonfire at her core. 'Which from this morning's evidence appears not to be a lie.'

She swallowed as the bonfire crackled and burned.

Why did knowing his response had been as genuine and unguarded as hers only make her feel more insecure? And more unsettled?

'I'd say that's not much of a basis for a marriage,' she said, before she could think better of it. She wanted to grab the words back when he sent a sharp glance her way.

'What did you say?'

'I said, I don't think that's much of a basis for a marriage,' she managed, knowing she'd said it now, so no more harm could be done by explaining herself. And anyway, she was tired of worrying about saying or doing the wrong thing constantly. Perhaps if they talked more, he'd realise she was doing her best. 'A shared love of horse racing, that is… And…' She coughed to dislodge the sudden blockage in her throat. 'And chemistry.'

His brows drew down as he approached the traffic lights at Hyde Park Corner. The Corinthian columns of Wellington Arch at the centre of the roundabout and the galloping horses of the bronze statue on top looked particularly imposing illuminated from beneath as the dusk descended over central London. But it was nowhere near as imposing as the silence in the car or the man beside her. Orla's pulse accelerated and the weight in her belly grew. She could sense his disapproval again—seemed she was getting very good at noticing that much about him, at least—but she refused to apologise. Being timid and self-effacing was not a good way to deal with Karim Khan, she decided, because it only gave him more power. And made her feel more useless. If she was going to get through tonight without making some major *faux pas* she was going to need his help... Instead of his disapproval.

'I would have to disagree,' he said at last, finally breaking the agonising silence. 'Chemistry was the *only* element that compelled my father to marry all four of his wives.'

His father had been married four times!

Shock came first, followed by a strange ripple of regret as she acknowledged the bitterness in his tone. No wonder this man had such a jaundiced view of love and relationships if that was his role model.

'Well, you might say that proves my point, rather than disproves it,' she countered.

The lights changed and he drove past the arch.

'How so?' he asked, as he shifted down a gear to accelerate around a delivery truck and make the turn onto Piccadilly.

'Perhaps if he'd considered more than chemistry when choosing a wife, he might not have had four of them.'

The minute the comment had left her mouth his lips drew into a tight line.

She wanted to bite off her tongue. Why couldn't she learn to keep her opinions to herself? Starting an argument with him was hardly the way to go here.

And his father's four failed marriages were

not her concern, any more than the bitter disillusionment in his tone was when he'd spoken of them.

But to her surprise, instead of telling her to mind her own business, his lips relaxed and he said, 'A good point. Although incorrect where my father is concerned.'

'How is that?' she asked, trying not to flinch when he sent her another assessing look.

Maybe he didn't want to talk about this, but she needed to know this stuff if she was going to pretend to be in love with him tonight with any degree of success.

Although her own parents' marriage had ended tragically, she could still remember the intimacy between them. Whenever they were together, it was the small possessive touches, the jokes only they shared, the secret looks they sent each other when they thought no one was watching, that announced their love, so much louder than any outward show of emotion or desire.

She suspected, from what Karim had just told her about his father's marriages and his scathing reaction to the L word yesterday, he would be unaware of how a connection like that manifested itself, so it would be up to her to fake that part… And there was no way she could do that if she didn't find out more about him. So surely the avid thundering of her pulse as she waited for him to give her an answer to her question was totally justified.

He sighed as if the question was an inconvenience rather than an intrusion, but when he spoke, she could hear more in his voice than impatience and it made her heart beat even harder.

'My father's reasons for marriage were twofold: sexual gratification and the production of male heirs. Only two of his wives managed to achieve the latter—my mother and my younger brother Dane's mother—but he grew bored with them all after a few years, at which point they were always discarded.'

The bland, almost bored tone as he described a man who sounded like an arrogant, entitled monster shocked her. But then the car crossed Piccadilly Circus, and the red and gold lights from one of the junction's illuminated advertising hoardings highlighted the tension in his jaw.

Was he really as unaffected by his father's behaviour, or just very good at hiding it?

'He doesn't sound like much of a husband… Or father,' she commented.

'He's not.' His lips twisted into a hard smile. 'But the only wives who suffered were the ones who made the mistake of believing he wanted more,' he added.

Did that include his mother? It was hard to tell from the flat, unsentimental tone.

'What about his children?' she asked softly.

He let out a harsh laugh. 'Dane and I survived without him,' he said.

He sounded unmoved, almost amused by the suggestion any child would need a father—she found his attitude unbearably sad. No wonder Karim Khan could view a relationship as nothing more than a business deal. But didn't every child deserve a father who cared for them as a person—as well as simply a means to continue their legacy? As difficult as it had been to watch her own father change after her mother's death, allowing the grief and eventually the gambling to destroy all their lives, he had loved and nurtured her and her sister once. What would it be like never to have that support?

The silence stretched between them again until a question formed in her mind.

'Won't you have to marry to provide heirs eventually too?' she asked, wondering how he was going to square that with his avowed decision never to do so. 'Being the Crown Prince?'

'My father certainly thinks so,' he said, the coldness in his voice chilling. 'I do not.'

He glanced at her as he flicked up the indicator to turn the car into Seven Dials.

'His attempts to force my hand in the matter

are the main reason I decided to acquire you, as it happens,' he added.

Orla blinked, his cynicism making her rub her arms despite the balmy summer evening.

So that was why he had needed a fake fiancée? To stop his father from trying to force him to marry. She supposed it made sense. But all it did was make her feel sadder for him. To have such a dysfunctional relationship with a parent—to know from a young age you had only ever been born for one purpose—couldn't be good for anyone.

But as he braked the car at the small roundabout in the middle of the Seven Dials, and handed his keys to a parking attendant, she tried to ignore the compassion tightening her throat and concentrate instead on the rigid line of his jaw.

Karim Khan, whatever the struggles of his childhood, was not the sort of man that inspired anyone's pity.

The road in front of The Chesterton Hotel had been closed off, and a red carpet laid on the centuries-old cobblestones flanked by a barrage of photographers. He escorted her through the mêlée, his hand once again doing diabolical things to her body temperature as the calluses skimmed across her naked back.

As they entered the hotel together, the anxiety in her gut twisted and burned and she forced herself to forget the glimmer of insight she had got into Karim's childhood during the drive.

Karim Khan wasn't an unloved boy, but a forceful, charismatic and extremely cynical man. Whatever had made him that man hardly mattered now, and she would do well to remember that. This wasn't a real relationship, despite the chemistry that had flared between them. It was a contract. And to hold up her end of the bargain, persuading everyone here she was the sort of woman Karim Khan, Crown Prince of Zafar, would choose to marry—was going to require an award-winning performance.

Unfortunately, getting to know more about Karim Khan hadn't helped at all in that endeavour—all it had done was make her feel even more out of her depth.

CHAPTER SIX

'WOULD YOU MIND if I went to the bathroom, Karim?'

At Orla's softly asked question, Karim turned from his conversation with a retired French champion jockey. Beneath the manufactured glow of affection, he could see the tiredness in her eyes and the strain around her mouth.

They'd been at the reception for over four hours, and she had played her role well. He had sensed her nerves at first, but he'd been impressed at her ability to talk with considerable knowledge and foresight about the business of racing. Even though she clearly hadn't socialised with the major players in the industry as he had originally assumed, she knew her stuff.

As the evening had progressed, though, it wasn't her knowledge of racing that had captivated him, but her attempts to appear the lovestruck fiancée. Where most women would have clung to his arm and fawned over him, she had blushed profusely every time anyone congratulated them on their engagement—which only made the story of their whirlwind courtship all the more credible.

In fact the charade had begun to feel so authentic he hadn't wanted to let her out of his sight.

And while the engagement might not be real, their physical connection had only become more tangible. The catch of her breathing every time he touched her and that instinctive shudder when he placed his arm around her waist to introduce her had begun to intoxicate him. But far worse had been the two times they had danced together and he had been forced to cut the experience short because her slender body, pliable and so responsive as she allowed him to lead, had a wholly uncontrollable effect on his as he pictured himself leading her in a very different dance.

All in all, the effect she had on him had become more disturbing as the evening progressed, making it next to impossible for him to keep his thoughts on what this engagement was actually supposed to achieve. And he wasn't happy about it, especially after the intrusive conversation they'd shared during the drive here.

He never normally responded to probing

questions about his family—not even from women he was dating. So why had he revealed so much about his relationship with his father? He'd refused to see the bastard in over a decade, refused to return to Zafar for considerably longer. And while he was happy to use his royal title, if it gave him an advantage in business, he had no intention of ever taking up the throne and took no interest in affairs of state. His father had cut him off financially when he was eighteen, after he had refused to marry or produce heirs—so why the hell had he told Orla about a relationship he no longer had any interest in?

But as Karim had begun introducing Orla as his fiancée, he'd begun to realise why he might have let so much slip in the car... Her frankness had beguiled him, as had the strange look in her eyes when he'd told her the truth about his father's marriages.

What the hell did that look even mean?

Because whatever it meant, he was beginning to appreciate the effect it had on him less and less. Especially as the urge to remain by her side grew, alongside the annoyance as he watched every other man there become captivated by her.

Since when had he had a jealous streak? Especially for a woman he hadn't even slept with?

He lifted his hand from Orla's waist, annoyed anew by his reluctance to let her out of his sight.

'Of course,' he said. 'Perhaps we should leave soon?' he added.

Wary surprise crossed her features. 'I... Yes, Karim,' she said. 'If you wish.'

Perversely, the subdued reply only irritated him more as she headed off through the crowd. Where was the woman who had kissed him with such passion that morning, or argued with him so persuasively in the car? More than a few men tracked her progress, and he felt the familiar surge of possessiveness—bordering on jealousy—that had dogged him all night.

'You are a man of considerable patience, Monsieur Khan,' the former jockey, whose name Karim had forgotten, remarked wryly.

'How so?' he asked, his gaze still fixed on Orla as she disappeared into the ballroom.

'If I had such a woman, I would want to keep her in my bed, rather than spend hours allowing other men to admire her charms.'

Karim swung round, the older man's comment making the heat—and frustration—he had been trying to control all evening surge. His fingers curled into fists, so he could resist the urge to punch the smile off the much smaller man's mouth.

'What did you say?' he snapped.

'There is no need to look so indignant, monsieur.' The jockey lifted his hands—palms up—in the universal sign of surrender, but the mocking, almost pitying, smile remained. 'I meant no offence to you or your fiancée.'

'Then what did you mean?' he growled, knowing he was overreacting, but not quite able to stop the outrage.

'Only that Mademoiselle Calhoun is exquisite—not just fresh and beautiful but also intelligent and accomplished. I am an old man, and I am jealous of you, for having so much to look forward to with such a woman by your side for the rest of your life.'

Karim frowned at the hopelessly romantic statement.

Not exactly, she will be gone as soon as she has outlived her usefulness.

Thanking the man through gritted teeth, he made his excuses and walked away, still furious at the presumptuous comment and the surge of frustrated desire it had caused.

His annoyance increased as he acknowledged the twist of regret in his stomach at the thought that Orla wasn't his. He headed towards the ballroom—where the dance floor was packed with people. Maybe Orla wasn't his. But he didn't want to watch any more men 'admiring' her charms. As soon as she reappeared they would leave.

Then perhaps he could calm down enough to

figure out how his fake fiancée had managed to complicate a perfectly simple business arrangement, tie his guts in knots, and turn him into a man he hardly recognised, in less than one night.

'Orla, dance with me...'

Orla barely had a moment to acknowledge the request before a damp palm clamped on her wrist and she was staring into a flushed freckled face she recognised.

'Patrick...!' She stiffened and reared back, as her former fiancé's now paunchy belly pressed into hers. But before she had a chance to extricate herself he had locked his other arm around her hips, like an iron band, and manoeuvred her onto the dance floor with him.

'Hello, Orla, don't you look good enough to eat...' His pale blue gaze dipped lasciviously to her breasts and his nostrils flared. A drop of sweat rolled down the side of his face to land on her shoulder. Funny to think that look had once made her feel special, when all it did now was make her flesh crawl.

She struggled, refusing to move her feet as he tried to sway with her in his arms.

'Patrick, let me go, you're locked,' she said, the stale scent of beer and whisky underlying the unpleasant smell of sweat.

She'd seen Patrick earlier in the crowd and had been beyond grateful he hadn't spotted her. But the truth was, she'd given him no more thought whatsoever, all her energies expended on dealing with the much bigger issue of not messing up the role she was playing for Karim tonight. And not letting any more of the destructive emotions that had assailed her in the car get the upper hand again.

As it happened, that hadn't been all that easy. Karim had remained by her side all night, which had only made her giddy, misguided reaction to him all the more intense and unpredictable. She'd tried to sound smart and authoritative when talking to racing industry figures she knew Karim had hired her to impress, her goal to persuade him she could do the job she'd begged him for the day before. But as the night had worn on and his unsettling effect on her had increased, she'd found it more and more difficult to string anything like a coherent sentence together.

Their dances together had been nothing short of excruciating. She didn't know how to dance, she hadn't socialised at all for five years and he had the smooth, easy grace of a man who was entirely in tune with his own body. The fact she been far too aware of every spot where their bodies touched had only made her more clumsy. As a result, he'd called a halt, not once but twice in the middle of the dance.

Not only was she failing at the job he was paying her for but the more attentive—and intense—he became, the more difficult she was finding it to remember this was a job at all.

The suggestion they leave soon should have brought some relief, but instead it had increased the melting sensation between her thighs and the pulse of panic that they were about to be alone again.

'Don't be so high and mighty, Orla,' Patrick said, bringing her sharply back to the present. He squeezed her so tightly she realised he wasn't just locked, he was loaded too, the outline of an erection pushing against her belly. Nausea rose up her throat, and she began to struggle in earnest to get away from him.

Sure she didn't want to create a scene, but Patrick was and had always been a jerk, and it humiliated her to think she had ever fancied herself in love with him.

Unfortunately, the more she struggled, the more he tightened his grip.

'Patrick, this isn't funny, you need to let me go.'

'Ah, shut up, now, Miss Priss,' he said. The old nickname, which she had once thought was affectionate but had become aware was just another way to belittle her, had the spike of temper igniting. 'Just because you've nabbed some foreign royal now.' His eyes narrowed to slits and his fleshy lips quirked, the cruel smile one she recognised, because it had once had the power to cut her to the quick. 'Does he know you're frigid yet?' he sneered. 'Or did you finally put out for someone?'

Anger flowed through her, to cover the cruel cut of inadequacy.

The urge to slap his face was swift and undeniable.

She'd be damned if she'd let Patrick Quinn make her feel like dirt again, when he was the one who had cheated on her. But as she jerked her hand loose from his embrace, a roar from behind had them both turning.

'Get your hands off my fiancée.'

Karim cut through the swathe of dancers like Moses parting the Red Sea. The fury on his face sent a shot of adrenaline through her system so swift it made her light-headed.

The too tight band of Patrick's arms released her so suddenly she stumbled.

Karim grabbed her elbow, his hand firm and dry as he drew her close and prevented her from falling on her face.

The giddy rush that had been messing with her equilibrium all evening surged up her torso, but as his gaze roamed over her—assessing her well-being as if he actually cared for her—it became even harder to deny, or control.

'Are you okay?' he demanded, his voice low with barely leashed fury. 'Did he hurt you? I saw him grab you, but I couldn't get to you fast enough.'

'No… I'm fine,' she said.

Patrick—who had always been a coward—had already fled.

Was this all part of their act tonight? The possessive Crown Prince, defending the honour of his new fiancée? She tried to convince herself, as she became aware of all the guests staring at them, but her pulse refused to cooperate, the giddy tattoo hammering against her ribcage as his gaze remained focussed solely on her. Almost as if he couldn't see anyone else. Which was madness, clearly, but no less intoxicating all the same.

How long had it been since anyone had looked out for her? Had taken account of her welfare? Had cared enough about her to ride to her rescue as Karim Khan just had?

'Wait here,' he said, the terrifying moment of connection lost as he let her arm go. 'I'm going to teach that bastard a lesson he won't soon forget.'

'No, don't, Karim,' she said, grasping hold of

his forearm, shocked when the muscle tensed beneath the sleeve of his jacket, sending a heady dart of delirious pleasure into her sex.

How could she be turned on? When this was a complete and utter disaster? Not only were they making a massive scene, but she was starting to lose her grip on reality. Not good.

'Pat's not worth it,' she added.

The frown became catastrophic again. 'Do you know that bastard?'

For a moment she debated lying to him. The last thing she wanted to do right now was talk about the man who had discarded her so callously all those years ago, when this man was making her feel even more needy. But she forced herself to tell him the truth.

'Yes. He's Patrick Quinn, the man I was engaged to,' she murmured, averting her face.

The light-headedness dropped into her stomach and turned her knees to wet noodles. A cold wave of shock mixed with the nerves to make the nausea rise up her throat as the reaction to Pat's assault set in.

'You're shaking.' Karim's deep voice seemed to come from miles away. 'Are you sure you're okay?'

'I think I'm going to be sick,' she blurted out.

'To hell with this,' he murmured, and she was scooped off the floor and into his arms.

'What are you doing?' she managed, as the scary feeling of being protected, cocooned, cherished wrapped around her torso.

It's not real, don't romanticise it.

But even as she tried to convince herself, she turned her face into his chest, to escape from the curious glances, the intrusive stares, that reminded her so much of that miserable April day when she'd had to announce to the engagement party her engagement was over.

'Getting us the hell out of here,' he growled as he marched through the crowd.

She pressed her nose into his collarbone, clung to his neck, and inhaled to give herself the moment she needed.

She breathed in his tantalising scent. The seductive aroma of soap and man cleared away the rancid smell of sweat and whisky.

At last the raging sea of shock and bitter memories calmed down.

But then his arms tightened around her, and the deep well of misguided emotion swelled into her throat.

What was she doing? Relying on his strength, even for a moment, would only make it harder for her to rely on her own. And that was one thing getting dumped by Patrick, losing her mother and then getting emotionally abandoned by her father had taught her, before she lost him too. Relying on anyone other than your-self would always lead to heartache.

So she shifted and tried to wiggle free of his arms. 'It's okay, Karim, really, I'm fine, you can put me down now.'

'In a minute.' Karim bit off the words, the rage still burning in his gut.

He walked down the steps of The Chesterton.

Patrick Quinn was going to regret touching her. Quinn and his whole damn family, when he buried their business.

His hands tightened reflexively, but he made himself place Orla on her feet. Even so he kept a firm grip on her arm as she steadied herself.

'How's the stomach?' he asked.

'Good,' she said, tugging away from him.

He forced his hand into his pocket to resist the urge to touch her again. And tried to convince himself his fury would be just as strong if Quinn had treated any other woman there the same way.

'It's okay, Karim, he didn't mean to hurt me, his hand slipped.'

A memory flickered at the edges of his consciousness, of his mother, her face pale but for the livid bruise on her cheek.

He shut it out, as well as the brutal feeling of impotence and inadequacy that came with it.

Orla wasn't his mother. She wasn't even really his fiancée. She meant nothing to him. And the surge of fury that had assaulted him in the ballroom when he had spotted Quinn dragging her onto the dance floor and seen her stiffen and recoil had not been specific, but rather a natural reaction to the sight of any man treating a woman with such disrespect.

'I'm sorry for the scene,' she said as she looked down at her toes.

'Don't apologise,' he said, more curtly than he had intended, the rage burning under his breastbone again. And feeling more specific by the minute. For a moment there she'd clung to him. And instead of being shocked or annoyed, all he'd wanted to do was hold her.

He signalled the parking attendant. He needed to calm the hell down.

This. Is. Not. Personal.

'You're not responsible for Patrick Quinn's boorish behaviour,' he added.

She met his gaze at last. 'Thank you,' she said.

'What for?' he asked, his pulse accelerating again, despite his best efforts. He hated to see the shadows in her eyes. Wanted nothing more than to take them away, even though it shouldn't matter to him, this much.

What was going on here? Because he didn't like it, but he didn't seem able to stop it.

'For coming to my rescue,' she said, so simply and with so little expectation, his heart squeezed uncomfortably in his chest. 'And for not blaming me.'

'Why would I blame you for his actions?' he asked. Did she think he was some kind of monster? A monster like his...

He cut off the thought. He didn't want to think about his father, especially not now—when the woman he had effectively hired to dupe the bastard had somehow duped him into feeling things he did not want to feel.

The car arrived before she replied, and he took a moment to tip the parking attendant and open the door for her. She climbed into the passenger seat, giving him another flash of her thigh. Her breasts rose and fell—making the glittery fabric of her gown shimmer erratically—and it occurred to him she wasn't any calmer than he was.

The inevitable shot of heat hit as he skirted the car and got behind the wheel. Just as he was about to switch on the ignition though, she murmured, 'I made such a mess of things tonight, I wouldn't blame you a bit for wanting to sack me.'

He stared at her—the urge to defend her so

swift and strong it was as confusing as everything else that had happened tonight.

But seriously, what on earth made her believe she had messed up? And at what exactly? Convincing people their engagement was real? Because she'd been too damn convincing at that, so convincing in fact he'd begun to believe it himself.

Even though a part of him knew he should take her up on her suggestion, and call a halt to this charade—because it had already become more complicated than it was ever meant to be—he couldn't do it.

So he turned on the ignition, peeled away from the kerb and asked the question that had been bugging him as soon as she had told him about her connection to Quinn.

'Why do you call him Pat? Do you still have feelings for that bastard?' Why the hell that should matter to him, he had no idea, but still, he wanted to know.

'Oh, no, not at all,' she said, the surprise in her voice and the instant reply mitigating at least some of his anger. 'The truth is I haven't thought about him in years.'

'How did it end?' Even as the probing question came out of his mouth, he knew he shouldn't have asked it—any more than he should want to know the answer. Her previous affairs were no business of his. But he'd be damned if he'd take it back.

Surely, he could be forgiven for being curious? After all, she had been engaged to that bastard when she was only seventeen. The man had most likely been her first lover.

He tapped his thumb on the steering wheel, jerked the gear shift into second to take the turn into Shaftesbury Avenue waiting for her reply—which didn't come nearly as quickly as her previous answer, he noted. His impatience mounted as the car sped past the row of theatres, their doors closed now, and the paper lanterns of Chinatown speckled light onto the hood.

'We were very young,' she said at last as he braked at the lights on the junction with Haymarket.

He glanced her way, hearing the hesitation in her voice.

'And we eventually figured out we just didn't suit,' she finished. But he could see the flags of vivid colour on her cheeks. She was lying, he was sure of it—there was more to it than that.

The questions cued up in his head.

How long were they together? Why did it really end? Had that bastard touched her roughly then too, the way he had tonight? But as the night air cooled at least some of the heat churning in his gut, he forced himself not to ask any of them.

Whatever had happened between Orla and Quinn in the past, once he had dealt with the man, Quinn certainly would not make the mistake of hurting her again.

And her past really did not concern him.

They made the rest of the drive in silence.

Unfortunately, as his fury began to cool, the hunger, and heat that had dogged him all night returned. He could sense the charge between them now like a living, breathing thing, and was sure she could feel it too.

Was it why he didn't want to let her go?

After he parked the car in the garage behind the house, she leapt out before he had a chance to open her door.

'Will you want me tomorrow?' she asked, backing away from him towards the house.

I want you tonight.

He cut the thought off, forced himself not to act on it. 'No,' he said.

Space and distance were necessary, until he could control his reaction to her in every respect.

'Would it be okay if I returned to Kildare for a few days, then?' she asked, the colour on her cheeks still vivid as her back hit the door.

'No, it would not be okay,' he said, a lot more

forcefully this time. Maybe space and distance were required, until they got this hunger under some semblance of control, but he'd be damned if he'd let her leave the country. 'We're supposed to be engaged, Orla,' he added. 'Leaving so soon won't fit the narrative.'

Nor would it improve his mood.

'But if you don't need me here, I'm sure there's lots I could be doing there...' Her breathing speeded up again and drew his gaze back to her cleavage, where the material shimmered and glowed and he could see the slope of her bare breast at the side of that damn gown that had been playing peek-a-boo with him all night... 'To brief your team when they—'

'I said no.' He interrupted the far too eager stream of suggestions. 'I'll be travelling to the stud next month, you can accompany me then. But I've already hired a new manager to take over the day-to-day running of the facility.'

'Oh.' She looked crestfallen. 'I see.'

He refused to feel guilty about it. This was what they'd agreed. She shifted out of his way as he approached the door—tense and skittish.

'I'll contact you when I require you to attend an event with me,' he said, trying to keep his mind on business and off the soft sway of her unfettered breasts.

She nodded. 'Okay. But what am I supposed to be doing in the meantime?' she asked.

He could think of far too many answers to that question. Every one of them only making the visceral need that had been riding him all evening increase, so his reply was sharp enough to make her jump.

'Waiting for my instructions.'

He unlocked the door and held it open for her, getting a lungful of that provocative scent for his pains that seemed to stroke the erection growing in his pants.

'Do you understand?' he asked.

He saw the mutinous expression in her eyes, and hated himself even more for noticing how it turned her irises to a rich emerald.

'Of course, Your Highness,' she said, but before he could take her to task for the mocking comment, she shot past him into the house.

He closed the door as he watched her disappear down the hallway.

The urge to go after her clawed at his gut. But just as vivid was the memory of her eyes—so wary, so vulnerable—as he'd carried her out of the ballroom. Something tightened in his chest as he remembered how she'd clung to him for that split second as trusting as a child.

As he made his own way through the dark

house, the antique grandfather clock in the vestibule chimed midnight.

Taking this any further would be a mistake.

Sex was one thing, intimacy another, and he would never risk mixing the two.

CHAPTER SEVEN

'ORLA, I CAN'T believe you're actually engaged to a prince—that's mad.' Dervla's shocked voice made Orla's fingers tense on her phone in the upstairs lounge. 'I mean, I know he's super-hot and all, but I didn't think you were actually serious.'

'Dervla, I told you we're not really dating,' Orla whispered, worried that the staff might overhear her. Although she suspected they had realised she and Karim were not a real couple by now. After all, they had to have noticed the two of them had never shared a bed and she'd been living in his house for a week. 'It's not a proper engagement,' she added, even though it didn't feel entirely in name only either any more.

Not after their first—and only—event together as a couple.

'But I saw the pictures of him carrying you out of the Jockeys' Ball. It's in all the magazines over here.' Dervla sighed. 'It looks so romantic.

Are you sure he hasn't fallen hopelessly in love with you by accident?'

Orla felt the familiar pang in her chest and swallowed down the foolish lump of emotion that had derailed her a week ago when he'd come to her rescue like an avenging angel... Or a protective fiancé. And the times she had run the memory of those moments through her head. But in the days since, it had become clear, whatever had happened that night, it wasn't going to be repeated. She'd hardly seen him—but for the two breakfasts they'd shared.

Karim had been distant and pragmatic both times she'd managed to catch him before he disappeared for the day, keeping any conversation to a minimum. And when he did speak to her, the discussion was about the horses, never anything more personal. He had been picking her brains for everything she knew about the sport and the stock at Calhouns. She'd found the two discussions they'd had surprisingly stimulating—Karim knew much more than she'd assumed, his decision to buy the stud and establish himself as an owner of superior bloodstock not a vanity project after all. As much as she had regretted having to sell her family business, she could see Karim was going to invest and build on the work they'd done there. That he had chosen to keep the Calhoun name had also pleased her. But those breakfast meetings had still been extremely disconcerting. She'd felt his gaze on her, and that masculine magnetism that had tripped her up before. The events at the Jockeys' Ball and even the one kiss they'd shared had played through her mind whenever she was with him—and the many hours she was not.

But it was three days now since she'd last seen him. And she'd felt the sharp sting of disappointment each morning as she'd walked into the breakfast room and found it empty.

She'd tried to be philosophical about that. It wasn't really him she missed, surely it was just that she felt so rootless here, her life in the last week so far removed from her daily routine in Kildare. When she'd agreed to this arrangement, she really hadn't factored in what it would mean to be the trophy fiancée of a man as rich and powerful as Karim Khan. She'd never felt so useless in her life. Not only did she miss the horses desperately, but Calhouns and the work there had given her life purpose and meaning, and it was clear she had no purpose or meaning here.

With no horses to exercise, no final demands to juggle, no stud business to deal with, no bank managers to placate or stalls to muck out, and no mention of any events to attend with Karim, she'd struggled to find anything to do. The house was run like a well-oiled machine, the staff so efficient all her offers to help out had been met with puzzled frowns followed by polite refusals.

The truth was, the yearning she felt when not seeing Karim at the breakfast table was probably just disappointment. Because without that shot of adrenaline to liven up her morning—and the chance to at least talk about the business she loved—she'd become unbelievably bored.

She had no idea what she was even doing here any more, or why Karim continued to refuse to allow her to return to Kildare.

'No, he hasn't fallen in love with me,' Orla murmured to her sister. She'd explained the circumstances of the engagement to Dervla a week ago—in the scant twenty minutes Karim had allowed her before they left—and every time she'd spoken to Dervla since. But Dervla didn't believe her.

Orla had always been the realist and Dervla the drama queen, but her sister's ludicrous romanticism—her determination to make this engagement something it wasn't—wasn't helping Orla keep everything in perspective.

As a result, she'd started screening her sister's calls—which was a pain. Because the conversations with Dervla, however aggravating her attitude towards the engagement, were one of the few bright spots in her monotonous days in London. She was desperate for news of what was going on at the stud, something she couldn't quiz Karim about—because he was never here.

'How's everything going at Calhouns?' she cut into Dervla's continued dreamy dialogue about how hot the photos of her and Karim were in her magazines. Time to change the subject before Dervla drove her totally nuts.

'Oh, it's marvellous,' Dervla said. 'They've started work on repairing and updating the stable block and the training facilities this morning. They even got an architect in to do designs for the remodelling. Can you believe it?' Dervla's voice was hushed with awe. 'I didn't even know there were architects for horse barns. Did you? It's gas.'

'Where are the horses while all this is going on?' Orla asked. She hadn't expected them to start work so soon. The stables had been in desperate need of repairs, that was true, but didn't the new manager know they had to be careful not to disturb the horses? These were thoroughbred, highly strung animals and any noise or disruption could seriously damage their—

'They're stabling them at the Quinns' until the work is finished,' Dervla interrupted Orla's panicked thoughts. 'They moved them all yesterday.'

'Oh, I see, that makes sense.' Orla frowned, the twist of disappointment in her belly making her feel small and petty. Why should she begrudge her neighbours the business, just because Patrick had acted so appallingly at the ball? Karim had no loyalty to her, not really, especially where his business was concerned. 'I expect the Quinns'll be glad of the business,' she added, knowing the family had struggled in recent years because their horses hadn't had the same results as Calhouns on the track.

'I expect they would if they still owned the place,' Dervla said.

'What?' Orla asked.

'Didn't I tell you already? Someone bought their business in a hostile takeover… And kicked them off the land. Two days ago.'

'No, you did not mention it,' Orla said, her fingers gripping the handset. How could Dervla have forgotten to mention something so important? The Quinns had been a premier Kildare racing family for generations, just like the Calhouns.

'Ah, damn, I meant to tell you all about it yesterday. It was all over the pub on Sunday night, happened very suddenly, Maeve said. Her husband works at Quinns, you know. Apparently they kept all the staff on. Even increased their wages as a loyalty bonus. Maeve said Dermot's pleased, he thought Patrick had been running the place all wrong for years. The new owner's already made improvements.'

'Who is the new owner?' Orla asked, shocked despite the fact she would have agreed with Dermot on Patrick's handling of the stud since he'd taken over.

'Didn't I tell you now, the best bit of gossip?' Dervla said, her voice rising with excitement.

'No, what?' Orla asked, thinking her sister was going to give her an aneurysm if she didn't get to the point.

'So no one knows who the new owner is for sure—it was all done in a secret sale. But the very next day, Carly, the new manager here, announced Calhouns horses were being rehoused there, during the remodelling, so everyone got to thinking, it must be *him*.'

'Him who?' Orla asked, thoroughly frustrated now. Why couldn't Dervla ever give her a straight answer about anything without dressing it up in loads of fanciful nonsense?

'Him as in your fiancé. Maeve and Dermot and everyone else think he's the new owner for sure.' Dervla's voice lowered with even more unnecessary drama. 'And that he probably did it for revenge—isn't that so cool?'

'Revenge for what now?' Orla asked, but the weight in her stomach had already begun to twist and turn at the memory of Karim's fury, and the words he'd ground out.

'I'm going to teach that bastard a lesson he won't soon forget.'

'Don't be dense,' Dervla cut back in. 'For revenge against Patrick Quinn, of course, for daring to put his hands on you at the ball. And you keep saying he doesn't love you.' Dervla scoffed. 'Why would he do such a thing if he wasn't mad about you?'

'That… It can't be true…' Orla said, so shocked she didn't know what to think let alone say—the weight in her stomach now dancing a jig. Would Karim really have done such a thing? He'd talked about retribution at the ball for Patrick's behaviour, in the heat of the moment, but he'd calmed down once they were in the car on the way home. And after she'd told him an edited version of her break-up with Patrick, he hadn't mentioned the incident, or her former fiancé, again.

What shocked her more though was the spurt of something heady and exciting at the thought he might have done such a thing for her. But as soon as she acknowledged the feeling, she felt ashamed of it.

If Karim really had done this, it wasn't because of his feelings for her, because he clearly didn't have any. He'd barely acknowledged her presence in the last week. She hadn't even seen him for three days now. In truth, he didn't even seem interested in maintaining the charade any more that they were actually an item.

And while it was true Patrick had been unnecessarily cruel to her all those years ago, cheating on her the whole time they were engaged, Karim knew nothing of that. Patrick might have behaved very badly at the ball too, but he'd been drunk. And yes, his family had blamed her for the breakdown of the engagement, but did they really deserve to lose a family business they'd spent years building because Patrick had had one too many whiskies?

'Well, I reckon it's true. And I think it's super romantic,' Dervla added, unhelpfully. 'It's just what Patrick deserves—he was never as good with the horses as you are. And he knew it, that's why he was so mean to you. And now he's out of racing for good. No one will give him a job if they think your fella won't like it. So he'll have to find something else to be bad at. At least you won't ever have to see him at another official event. Are you sure you don't know anything about it? I told Maeve I'd ask you.'

It took several minutes of deflecting Dervla's increasingly probing questions, but Orla finally managed to get her sister off the phone. She put the receiver down, her fingers trembling as the confusion and anxiety built under her breast-bone and began to tangle with the weight in her stomach.

Surely Karim couldn't have done something so… Well, so vengeful? And for a woman he didn't really care about. It made no sense. But even as she tried to reassure herself, her heart began to beat two to the dozen.

Should she ask him? If he had bought Quinns? How could she not? And yet how did she even bring up a question like that? When the last thing she wanted to do was discuss Patrick with him again? And, anyway, when was she even likely to see him next?

She stared at the phone she'd been given by his personal assistant a week ago, a phone that was supposed to alert her to any events she might need to attend with Karim. The phone that hadn't rung or buzzed once since he'd in-sisted she stay in London—and then given her nothing to do.

She picked it up and scrolled through the numbers stored in the contacts. There were only two. One listed Khan—which had to be Karim. And the other with the name of the personal assistant. She didn't quite have the guts to ring Karim and ask him outright. But would it be so wrong to find out from the personal assistant where he was today?

She called the number. The assistant picked up on the second ring.

'Ms Calhoun, what can I do for you?' he asked politely.

'Hi, I was just wondering where Mr Khan is today?' she asked before she lost her nerve.

'Would you like me to give him a message?' the PA asked, rather evasively, she thought. Had he been instructed not to tell her Karim's whereabouts?

Damn.

'No that's fine, I have his number here, but I didn't want to disturb him if he's busy,' she said. 'Is he? Busy?' she added, then felt like a fool. Of course Karim was busy, he was always busy, the man ran a multibillion-dollar business empire, single-handedly from what she could gather given the amount of time he spent out of the house or locked in his study.

She was just debating whether to hang up, when the PA replied.

'We're going to be at Hammonds Sale this afternoon in Kensington Palace Gardens, which kicks off at three, so I would suggest contacting Mr Khan before it starts as he will be bidding on the lots.'

She thanked the man and then hung up.

Her heartbeat accelerated into her throat, the familiar tangle of nerves jumping and jiggling in the pit of her belly joined by the definite spike of irritation.

Karim had gone to Hammonds Sale without her? If he was planning to buy any stock there, why hadn't he taken her with him? She was the one who knew the horses Calhouns would need to buy, better than anyone.

She glanced at her watch.

A quarter to two. Instinct and the definite bubble of excitement drowned out the jangle of nerves and the prickle of irritation. She picked up the house phone and ordered one of the cars to be brought round to take her to the event.

She'd never had the chance to go to Hammonds Sale but she had always wanted to. They held it every year in the grounds of Kensington Palace. Everyone who was anyone in racing would be there and, while most of the big sales happened in private, occasionally there were some good horses up for auction. She'd forgotten it was today, probably because she'd forgotten what day it was entirely. But she had studied the catalogue herself months ago when it had been issued, as she did every year, imagining what it would be like if she had money to invest. She could give Karim her advice about the best prospects, and maybe... *Maybe* she'd get up the courage to ask him about Quinns. But more importantly, it was way past time she stopped sitting on her backside and waiting for Karim to give her something to do.

She rushed out of the study and up the stairs to her suite, to hunt through her wardrobe of new clothes and find something fancy enough to wear for the super-posh event.

As she stepped into the car half an hour later, her fingers trembled round the clutch purse she'd found in the wardrobe. Then the jumps and jiggles settled low in her abdomen and began to throb at the prospect of seeing Karim again.

She ignored them. Her excitement wasn't about Karim, and her ludicrous over reaction to him, it was about this chance to prove to him that while she might be hopeless as a fake fiancée she could be a real asset when it came to buying bloodstock for Calhouns.

'You drive a hard bargain, Khan. But one I think we will both benefit from immensely. Your knowledge of bloodstock is much better than I anticipated. More champagne?'

'I'm good, thanks.' Karim declined the offer of a top-up from Piers Devereaux—a racing legend who had established himself as the premier stud owner in England—and dismissed the condescending tone.

He had expected as much from doyens of the racing establishment such as Devereaux—which was precisely why he had spent several years doing his homework and waiting for the perfect purchase before making an assault on the higher echelons of the sport. The prestigious racehorse sale organised by Hammonds each year was a gala event. The auction itself was more of a social occasion than a business opportunity, because the real business was done as the movers and shakers chatted privately over vintage champagne and cordon bleu canapés. Karim had prepared carefully for this event, knowing he wanted to match Calhouns' top stallion Aderyn with one of Devereaux's mares. But as he listened to Devereaux, a question that had been tormenting him consistently for a week tormented him again. Given all his careful planning over the last few years to enter this arena, why the hell had he been so damn impulsive when choosing a fake fiancée? And why hadn't he brought Orla with him to this event? When she knew so much about Calhouns stock?

'I have heard your father has an amazing stock of thoroughbreds, but I never knew you were so interested in the Sport of Kings,' Piers continued. 'So what's the story on Quinns?' the older man asked bluntly. 'Did you destroy them as penance for young Pat's diabolical treatment

of your new fiancée—and his former fiancée—
as everyone believes?'

Karim clenched his teeth and held onto his
temper, with an effort. Devereaux was the first
person to have the audacity to actually ask the
question. But he wasn't the first to think it.
Hammonds was buzzing with the latest gossip—he'd noted the questioning glances as soon
as he'd arrived. But he'd be damned if he'd explain or deny his actions to these people. Taking
over the Quinn farm had been a sound business
move, once he'd discovered they were ripe for
a takeover.

But even as he told himself that, he knew it
wasn't the whole truth.

Destroying Patrick Quinn's standing in the
community had been more than business. And
he'd been trying to justify the impulse to himself ever since.

'The Quinn land borders on Calhouns, and
I intend to expand the operation considerably,'
he answered calmly, deciding not to deny he
was the new owner. 'Figure out my motives for
yourself.'

Maybe his motives had more to do with
Orla—and the sight of her being manhandled
by that bastard—than they should. But he refused to regret the impulse. No woman deserved
to be touched without her consent.

Devereaux chuckled, as Karim knew he would, because loyalty came a distant second to power and success in this community. 'Touché, Khan. Now I've met you, it's clear the rumours circulating about your hot-headedness are unfounded.'

Karim ignored the familiar prickle of unease at the comment. A week ago, Devereaux would have been correct. He'd never been a hothead, and certainly not over a woman, until he'd met Orla Calhoun. And he'd never had a problem controlling his impulses or his temper, but now he couldn't seem to keep a handle on either of them. And he didn't like it.

'I'm looking forward to working with you and competing against you,' Devereaux added. 'With Calhoun stock and your own considerable expertise you could well become a force to be reckoned with in a few years. Such a shame Michael passed when he did. The man knew horses like no other, even if he had trouble passing a betting shop.'

Karim bristled at the latent sexism of the man's assumptions. His in-depth conversations with Orla earlier in the week had proved to him conclusively she hadn't lied about her influence at Calhouns in the last few years. Although the racing community were blissfully unaware of her talents, it wasn't her father who had managed to steer Calhouns to so many successes despite the crippling debt the man's addiction had landed her with.

Thoughts of Orla though awakened the familiar pulse of yearning. Infuriatingly.

He'd been avoiding her for three days now. Ever since their impromptu breakfast meetings had given him a burning desire that had nothing whatsoever to do with mining her extensive knowledge of Calhouns' strengths and weaknesses.

How could he still want her so much? Even more now than he had the night of the ball? Why was the hunger only getting worse? And why couldn't he control it?

Almost as if he'd conjured her up by magic, his fiancée appeared at the tented opening to the event. He blinked several times. Was he hallucinating now? This was intolerable—weren't the dreams of her every damn night since she'd arrived in his home enough?

But as his gaze locked on her slender, willowy figure and high breasts, displayed to perfection in a floaty, fluid sundress the same rich, striking green as her eyes, it became clear she was not an apparition.

The moment of relief though—that he wasn't going totally insane—was followed by the bru-

tal shaft of heat. He tensed, furious with the unbidden and uncontrolled reaction.

What was she doing here? He certainly had
not requested her presence, for precisely this
reason. Because she distracted him. A lot.

But even knowing he ought to fight the disturbing effect she had on him, he found himself
tuning out Devereaux's small talk as he watched
her pick her way across the grass in her heels.
She kept her head down, and her hands gripped
the auction brochure she had been handed when
she entered. She declined the offer of a glass of
champagne from a passing waiter, pausing to
look around.

He resisted the urge to go to her immediately,
attempting to swallow down the ball of lust…
Not very successfully.

*Calm down, dammit. She'll spot you in a min-
ute and then you can demand to know what she
is doing here.*

Looking too eager was not his style, and having a domestic dispute in full view of everyone
would hardly keep up the pretence that he was
in love with this woman.

But as he battled the desire to storm through
the crowd—and reignite the rumours about his
being a hothead where this woman was concerned—a young man in a designer suit waylaid
her. Orla paused, clearly disconcerted by the at-

tention, especially when her admirer began to flirt with her in that way the English aristocracy had of being loud and annoying and thinking it was charming.

The possessive rage that had blindsided him at the ball a week ago surged.

And he had the answer to a question he hadn't even acknowledged... Avoiding her hadn't worked, if anything it had only made the hunger, and the inexplicable emotions that went with it—jealousy, envy, need—all the more volatile.

He made his excuses to Devereaux, dumped his empty glass on the tray of a passing waiter and headed towards his fiancée, ready to extricate her from the attentions of that obnoxious toff who had his eyes glued to her cleavage.

'So you're Irish? I should have guessed from the charming accent. And the red hair.' The young man grinned flirtatiously as his gaze finally lifted from Orla's breasts to her face. 'Are you dating one of the Irish breeders, then?' he said, putting enough emphasis on the word breeders to be less than charming.

She tried not to be insulted. While racing had always been a male-dominated sport, women were making their mark as both breeders and trainers, so this idiot's assumption that she was some airhead who knew nothing about the sport had just given away his ignorance.

'No, I'm Orla Calhoun, of the Calhoun stud…'

'Orla, you're here.' Her explanation of who she was dried up as Karim appeared from nowhere. Dressed in a grey linen suit, he looked dominant and powerful and stupidly gorgeous. So what else was new?

Heat suffused her cheeks, and sank deep into her sex, as he clasped her elbow in strong fingers. 'This is a surprise,' he said, the edge in his voice unmistakeable.

He didn't sound too pleased to see her, but before she could reply he pressed his lips to her cheek in a fleeting but somehow possessive kiss.

Fire ignited in her belly and spread up her collarbone.

It was the first time he had touched her since the ball. His dark gaze seared her skin, the intensity so vivid and compelling it felt as if they were alone—cocooned by the live-wire chemistry that flared between them so easily.

The jiggle of nerves she had tried to explain away during the drive to West London became turbocharged. Why did she feel as if she had just been branded? How did he do that? Make her feel as if she belonged to him? When she knew she didn't?

'Um, Karim, hi,' she managed, clearing her throat while desperately trying to get her bearings again—and remind herself that she was here to prove to him she could be useful. 'I heard you were at the auction and thought you could use my help with the bidding,' she managed, desperately trying not to get derailed again by his disapproval. He should have invited her, why hadn't he?

The young man beside her cleared his throat obviously waiting for an introduction.

'Karim, this… This is, um…' She turned to the young man, but even though he had introduced himself to her less than five seconds ago, his name totally escaped her.

'Miles, Miles Johnson at your service,' he said and offered his hand to Karim, managing to collect himself quicker than she had.

Karim merely glanced at the offered hand, which was hastily withdrawn. 'Hello,' he said.

'I'm honoured to meet you, Your Highness,' the boy continued—for he suddenly seemed like a boy rather than a man as his confidence visibly disintegrated under Karim's focussed disdain. 'E-everyone's t-talking about y-your acquisition of Quinns,' he stammered. 'What a bold move that was. And how you're set to be the most exciting thing to happen to racing in years…'

Orla shivered. So Karim *had* bought out the Quinns. And he hadn't bothered to tell her. All the questions she'd had before about the purchase came hurtling back, along with that weird feeling of vindication.

'Are they really?' Karim remarked, but he already sounded bored.

His thumb stroked her inner elbow, the light touch controlling enough to send her heartbeat catapulting into her sex.

'Yes, sir, they—' Miles began again. But this time Karim cut him off.

'Miles, do you think you could leave us alone? I'd like to speak to my fiancée in private.'

'Your fiancée?' The boy's face went bright red, but it was the flash of panic in his eyes that spoke volumes. 'I'll be off, then,' he said and left so fast Orla felt sure the rumours Dervla had repeated about Karim's motivations for destroying the Quinns, while they couldn't be true, had certainly travelled far and wide in the racing world.

'That's quite a trick,' she murmured, aware of the flicker of panic in her own body—but for very different reasons—as Karim pulled her round to face him.

'What trick?' he asked as he drew her closer, so close she could smell his cologne, and the subtle scent of his soap, which had haunted her dreams for days.

'The ability to make annoying people disappear. I wish I had that knack,' she said.

The slow smile that curled his lips was so sensual and so arrogant her breathing became distressingly ragged. 'I'll teach you it,' he said. 'But first you need to answer a question for me.'

'Yes,' she said, fairly sure they weren't talking about Miles What's-His-Name anymore.

'What the hell are you doing here?'

The question was delivered calmly but with enough of an edge for Orla to know he was holding onto his temper for the benefit of their audience. But while the nerves in her belly were now doing back flips she refused to apologise. He'd left her alone for a whole week, with nothing to do. After refusing to let her return to Kildare. She needed a role in London, or she'd go mad.

'I knew my knowledge of the lots could be useful. I've studied the catalogue and I know what Calhouns needs to purchase...' The frantic explanation trailed into silence as he continued to stare at her. One dark brow rose up his forehead, making his scepticism clear. And suddenly she found herself blurting out, 'Why did you buy out the Quinns? And destroy Patrick's reputation? Was it...?' She sucked in a breath, determined to continue despite the way both his brows lowered ominously—this was not a conversation he wanted to have. But she needed to know. 'Was it because of what happened at the ball?'

'You think I spent fifteen million euros to buy a stud farm neighbouring Calhouns to defend your honour?' he asked.

The mocking tone and the glitter of cynicism in his eyes were unmistakeable. But she could still detect that edge. And before she could stop herself she asked the question that had been burning in her gut since her conversation with Dervla. 'Well, did you?'

The minute she'd said it, she felt like a fool. Of course he hadn't—why would he really care about that, if he didn't care about her?

The rueful smile remained fixed on his lips, but his eyes narrowed.

'No,' he said.

Her chest deflated, and hot colour flared in her cheeks, making her feel hideously exposed. But then he stroked the side of her face with his thumb, the callused skin sending darts of sensation everywhere. His touch was light but so intimate her breath caught when he added, 'Or not entirely.'

She gulped down the lump forming in her throat. And began to feel light-headed. Was it the intensity in his gaze? That misguided yearning to be sheltered and cherished by this man—

that had overwhelmed her when he had rescued her from Patrick that night? Or was it the visceral desire tugging at her sex and making every one of her pulse points pound? Because she was fairly sure the excitement racing through her veins right now wasn't to do with her desire to find a way to be useful when it came to buying bloodstock for Calhouns anymore.

The stunned awareness in Orla's eyes turned the bright emerald to a compelling jade and sent a renewed shaft of longing through Karim's system… And he was finally forced to confront the lie he'd been telling himself for a week, that somehow by avoiding her he would be able to control the effect she had on him.

He'd never gone back on a contract, never reneged on an agreement. That wasn't how he did business. But this had stopped being a business deal a week ago. This was about need and desire and chemistry as well as expediency now.

This hunger was visceral and real and all-consuming. For them both. And if they didn't feed it soon it would only become more so.

He could hear the speeches being made by the director at Hammonds and then the auction began. The auctioneer listed the first horse up for sale: a two-year-old filly who had run some good races.

Orla's gaze flickered away from his face. She looked down at the brochure in her hands, avoiding his eyes. 'You should buy her. She's a good prospect.' She flicked through the pages, her fingers trembling. 'And number five, Debonair Boy, is a good colt,' she said, her cheeks glowing as she struggled to fulfil the role he'd once given her... A role that he now didn't give a damn about. It wasn't her expert racing advice he wanted. If it had ever been.

He signalled to his assistant, who was hovering nearby. The man appeared by his side instantly. 'Jason, buy this filly. And the fifth horse on the docket,' he said, not taking his gaze off his fiancée.

'Yes, Mr Khan,' the man replied.

'And make my excuses to Devereaux,' he added, surprised he could even remember the commitment he'd made earlier when all he could seem to focus on was the staggered rise and fall of Orla's breathing, the sultry scent of her perfume and how much he wanted to strip her out of the summer dress and lick every inch of her fragrant flesh. 'I won't be joining him for dinner after all.'

His assistant nodded and left. Karim gripped Orla's elbow and began to direct her through the crowd, back towards the entrance she'd come out of less than fifteen minutes before.

'Karim, is everything okay?' she asked, the nervousness in her voice only making him more aware of the arousal darkening her gaze.

'No, everything's not okay,' he managed. 'But it soon will be.'

He walked past the cloakroom set up by the entrance. 'Wait, Karim, I left my—'

'I'll get Jason to collect it,' he snapped. He could feel her pulse battering his thumb as he pressed it into the soft inner flesh of her elbow—trying not to grip her too hard.

'Tell my driver we're ready to leave,' he said to one of the doormen.

'But, Karim, we're going to miss the auction,' Orla said, then chewed her damn lip.

His gaze fixed on the plump flesh trapped between small white teeth. The desire to touch his tongue to the reddened skin was so strong he spoke through gritted teeth.

'Are there any more horses you think we should bid on?' he asked.

She shook her head, but the flush of pleasure—because he had asked for her advice—only made him feel more on edge.

'Good,' he said. 'Then there is no need for us to remain here.'

He stood on the grassy verge at the entrance to Kensington Gardens waiting for the chauffeur-driven Mercedes to arrive, aware of her starting to tremble beside him. He probably ought to reassure her. But how could he, when he couldn't even reassure himself?

He was behaving like a madman, the way he had at the ball. But he couldn't wait any longer to get this damn desire out of his system. Why hadn't he done this a week ago? Or any of the nights since? Instead of torturing himself for days? He would be over this driving hunger now if he had… Surely.

The car pulled into the park gates what felt like several eternities later.

After they were finally inside, cocooned in the leather interior, he tapped on the driver's window. 'Take us back to the house, Mark, park in the back and don't disturb us.'

The driver nodded, then closed the partition.

Finally they were alone. The spurt of adrenaline—and anticipation—had his heart beating heavily as the car drove off.

'Are you angry that I came?' she asked as she reached for her seat belt.

'No,' he said. 'Come here,' he added, gripping her arm before she could anchor the belt.

He dragged her up, and over him, until she straddled his lap. Her knees dug into the leather on either side of his hips, her fingers grasped his shoulders and the colour on her face intensified as he ran his hands up her thighs, felt the shudder of reaction. And caught the musky scent of her arousal.

Shock flickered across her face, but did nothing to lessen the vivid desire he could see in her eyes. Or the rush of blood pounding into his pants and thickening his shaft.

'Karim, what are you doing?' she gasped.

He caressed the glorious curve of her bottom through her panties and tugged her closer to murmur against the pummelling pulse in her neck: 'Changing the terms of our agreement.'

CHAPTER EIGHT

NEED RUSHED THROUGH Orla's system like wild-
fire, scorching everything in its wake, the hard
press of his erection against her thigh only in-
creasing the giddy sense of desperation—and
validation—at his murmured comment.

His thumb glided beneath the leg of her panties, finding the slick seam of her sex as his lips
devoured her neck, her collarbone.

'Tell me you want me, too,' he growled, his
voice a husky rasp of command.

'Yes, yes, I do,' she said.

'This changes nothing,' he said as he deftly
undid the buttons at the front of her dress, ex-
posing the white lace bra. 'Tell me you understand that.'

She nodded, unable to speak now, the anticipation starting to choke her as she heard the
snap of her bra releasing in the quiet interior
of the car.

They struggled for a moment, as he adjusted

her on his lap, so he could release her arms from the confines of the dress, and free her breasts.

Her nipples throbbed, so hard they were already begging for his attention.

She sat on his lap, topless and exposed and so needy she thought she might actually die from the desperate need to feel his lips on her. The solid erection felt huge trapped between her legs, but only increased her desire. She wriggled, instinctively trying to alleviate the pressure against the hard ridge.

He groaned, the raw sound a sop to her ego, making her feel powerful... Or at least less powerless.

His dark eyes met hers as he cradled the swollen weight of her breasts in his palms, traced the edges of the areolae. 'Don't move, Orla. Or this will be over far too soon.'

She stilled, the agony intensifying.

Then he bent forward and licked across the turgid tip of one nipple. She moaned, bucked, unable to do as he demanded, rubbing against the ridge trapped in his pants. The exquisite torture continued as he captured the stiff peak with his mouth and suckled hard. The pressure built and twisted at her core, her skin tight, raw, aching, her breasts on fire as he tormented one nipple, then the other.

Her soft, guttural moans echoed around the car, flagrant, uninhibited, desperate.

He bucked his hips, and finally released her from the torture, rearing back to press his hands to her burning cheeks.

'Release me,' he said.

She nodded, eager and yet unsure. Aware of him watching her, she tried to look as if she knew what she was about as she fumbled with his zip, concentrating hard. At last she managed to locate the tab and draw it down, her fingers shaking. As she undid the zip, revealing black boxer briefs, the defined outline of his erection took her breath away.

Good Lord, that's... Impressive.

She pulled the waistband down and the erection leapt free, so hard, so long, so thick, so beautiful.

Her breathing clogged in her lungs, the air conditioning chilling her damp breasts only adding to the barrage of sensations as she stared at the magnificent length.

Had she done that to him? Did he want her that much?

'Does it hurt?' she said, then realised her mistake when he gave a strained chuckle.

'Yes, it does. I'd love nothing more than for you to ride me right now,' he said, the explicit language only making her feel more needy, more desperate and like more of a fraud. 'But I don't have protection with me. So we'll have to be creative.'

She wanted to ask his permission, to touch him, but forced herself to trail a finger down the solid length, gasping when it jumped, bending towards her touch.

'Hold me,' he said, his voice a tortured husk of breath. It was all the encouragement she needed, fascinated and so turned on her thoughts were no longer her own.

She wrapped trembling fingers around the thick girth, marvelling at how soft and strong he felt—like steel encased in the finest velvet. Her thumb captured the bead of moisture leaking from the crown, lubricating her fingers, allowing her to slide them up, then down.

'Ah, yes…' He shuddered, shifted. The feeling of power built but then he moved the hand he still had in her panties. She bucked against his hold, his touch sure and firm and unflinching as he pressed the heel of his palm into her vulva then teased the swollen nub. He circled and stroked, expertly stoking the fire until it burned and stung.

But even as the rush of desire hit her, so did the terrifying rush of emotion.

'Tell me what you want,' he demanded.

So many things, too many to count.

'I…'

I don't know…

'Is this good?' he asked.

She nodded, round a choking sob, just as he swirled and stroked over the very heart of her.

She jolted, panting now, trying to concentrate on him, but too aware of his devious, devastating touch. She was caught in a battle of power, and passion and submission. A battle she was desperate to wage, but soon realised she didn't know how to win.

For while her movements became more clumsy, his were sure and true—torturing, tantalising, tormenting her.

She bowed back, forced to release her hold on him as the shattered sobs gathered in her lungs. The waves were building too fast for her to breathe, to think, to concentrate, to focus on anything but the tumultuous swell of pleasure. She moaned as the pulsing heat rose up from her core like a tsunami, destroying everything in its path.

He planted a hand on her back to bring her forward, to suckle her nipple, deep into his mouth at the exact moment the wave crashed through her.

She cried out, seeming to ride on the crest for what felt like an eternity. His fingers driving her up, and over, again.

At last she collapsed against him. Tears stung her eyes and she blinked them back furiously.

Don't cry, or he'll know you've never done this before.

'Shh…' he murmured against her cheek. He gathered her hair in a tail with one hand and gently tugged, forcing her to raise her head, so he could stare at her with those dark eyes.

But where she had expected to see accusation, disgust—she hadn't upheld her part of the bargain after all, had left him wanting—instead a sensual smile curved his lips.

'Are you okay?' he asked.

'Yes, that was…' she had no words, she realised '…really hot.'

He barked out a laugh.

'Good,' he said. 'Because it was really hot to watch.'

'You're not angry?' she blurted out, still confused by his reaction.

His shaft was still so hard, so huge, pressed into her belly.

Patrick had been furious with her, when she had failed to get him off once, while they necked. Although that had been nothing like this. Patrick had never touched her, or tasted her the way Karim had, had never even seen her naked, or semi naked. But he'd told her men had expectations, surely Karim would have them too—why wasn't he mad at her? For prioritising her own pleasure?

'Are you joking?' he said. The puzzled frown only made him look more seductive and made her feel more insecure.

'I didn't…' She glanced down, seeing the hard length still trapped between them. 'I didn't take care of you.'

He chuckled, the sound strained but no less amused. The sound reverberated off the leather seats, making her both painfully embarrassed, but also strangely comforted. At least he definitely wasn't mad with her.

'You're such a surprise,' he said when the chuckles had finally stopped.

For a heartbeat, maybe even two, she thought she saw genuine affection in his eyes, as he ran a thumb down the side of her face and stared into her eyes. Her heart swelled painfully into her throat, with a yearning far stronger than the one she'd just experienced.

'It's not an obligation, Orla. Or a race. We can easily remedy that once we're in a bed and I can take you properly. This was just a taste. Suffice it to say, what you did do will probably keep me hard until then.'

She nodded, the yearning, and the fear that went with it, starting to choke her.

Don't need more from him, Orla. Don't you dare. This is just sex. No biggie.

The sudden tap on the door had them both jumping. It was only then she realised the car had stopped moving. When had that happened?

Mortification hit and she scrambled off his lap, trying to tug up her dress.

Karim chuckled again before shouting, 'Mark, I told you not to disturb us.'

He readjusted his own clothing, with a non-chalance that suggested how commonplace the experience they'd just shared must be for him. She tried not to let it derail all her happy thoughts, or the endorphins still charging through her system.

He probably turned women to mush in the back seat of his limo every other day of the week. Didn't mean this couldn't be special, precious, for her.

Still just sex, remember.

'I'm sorry, Your Highness, it's not Mark, it's Muhammed,' came the reply from outside the car. 'We have just received urgent news from Zafar. News I thought you should hear immediately.'

The atmosphere in the car changed, a dark frown marring Karim's brow, the smile dying on his lips. 'Okay, wait there.'

He glanced at her as she struggled to do up her bra. 'Do you need help?'

'No, I'm... I'm grand,' she said as the damn thing finally snapped into place, the mortification starting to outweigh the endorphins.

He nodded, then, grasping her neck, he tugged her towards him for a kiss.

'Stay here,' he said. Then opened the door. He slammed it shut again after stepping out of the car and she acknowledged the pulse of regret that, whatever had just happened between them...nothing had really changed. She still wasn't an important part of his life. Certainly not important enough to know what had put that dark frown on his face.

But as she buttoned the front of her dress, her nipples still raw from his ministrations, she could overhear the conversation outside.

'What is it, Muhammed?' Karim commanded. 'I told you I don't receive my father's calls and I don't want to be bothered with his messages or demands.'

'I'm sorry, Your Highness,' the butler replied. 'But this was a message from the head of Zafar's Ruling Council. The news will be released tomorrow morning to the world's press, but Mr Abdallah wished to inform you immediately, your father died twenty minutes ago, and you are now the new King of Zafar.'

CHAPTER NINE

'KARIM, HOW ARE YOU?'

Karim looked up from his desk to see Orla silhouetted in the doorway of his study.

Heat surged, inevitably, making him tense, but the sight of her also lifted the weight that had been sitting on his chest since yesterday, ever since he had walked away from her—and into a nightmare.

'Good,' he lied.

He dropped the papers he had been reading—the contents of which had begun to blur in front of his eyes about half an hour ago—and thrust his fingers through his hair. He hadn't slept in close to thirty-six hours. Probably not the best time to have her in his office.

Orla was a problem, just like every other damn thing in his life right now, and he still hadn't decided what to do about her. By rights he didn't need her any more—or their fake engagement—his father was dead. And he was going to have to take his place on the throne, for the next few months at least—which meant he was being forced to return to Zafar tomorrow.

He had sworn he would never return to the desert kingdom, had never intended to succeed his father. But the old bastard had had the last laugh, his untimely and unexpected death at only sixty making it impossible for Karim to escape the responsibility.

A delegation had arrived that morning from Zafar, explaining that a constitutional crisis would engulf the country if he did not take his place on the throne. His father had ruled Zafar for years with an iron fist—as a result the institutions of state, including the Ruling Council, were no longer fit for purpose. Karim planned to bring democratic rule back to the kingdom, as soon as possible, but until that was done—and it could take months, given the state of the country's infrastructure and institutions—he would have to be a monarch in a lot more than name.

As she stood on the threshold of his study, the spark of attraction—and something more, that strange yearning that seemed to go beyond the physical—spread through his system.

Leaving his life behind in the UK, turning the management of his businesses over to his board while he concentrated on freeing Zafar from his father's brutal legacy, was going to be tough enough. But more than that, it wasn't going to be easy to explain Orla's sudden disappearance to the council members he'd spoken to that morning, who had suggested the engagement was something that would move the country forward.

Of course, he knew it wouldn't, because it was not going to lead to marriage, but ending it so abruptly and sending Orla back to Kildare might well be premature.

'What time is it?' he asked, his voice husky to his own ears as he got up from the desk and moved towards her. 'Shouldn't you be in bed?'

'I couldn't sleep,' she said. 'I just wanted to come and check you were okay. And give you my condolences.'

'What for?' he asked, his mind groggy as he took in the simple jeans and T-shirt she wore. When had her tomboy attire become so damn appealing? The memory from yesterday, the echo of staggered sobs, the feel of her flesh, slick, swollen, ready for him as the orgasm he controlled ripped through her body, assailed him all over again. When had everything about her begun to intoxicate him?

Had it always been so? He wondered, his tired mind not quite able to figure out a coherent answer. His hand lifted out of his pocket, the urge to touch her again unstoppable, but then she turned into the light.

'For your father, Karim,' she said, the deep well of compassion in her eyes making him stiffen and drop his hand. 'I'm so sorry for your loss.'

The brutal feeling of exposure at the softly spoken words washed through him like acid. He wanted *her*, not her pity.

He shrugged, the movement stiff. 'Don't be, I'm not.'

If she was appalled by the bitter remark, she didn't show it, her gaze still containing that tender glow—almost as if she could see into his soul and knew he was lying.

He shouldn't want her compassion, shouldn't care about the sympathy she offered. He had not loved his father; he certainly wouldn't miss the man, and he had survived very well without anyone's care or compassion since he was a child of ten. So why on earth should he respond to that look now? Or be comforted in some weird way by the simple fact of her presence in his home? He hadn't spoken to her since hearing of his father's death, although he'd thought about her often while being inundated with the responsibilities involved in sorting out his business affairs to make tomorrow's trip.

'You should go to bed,' he said, keeping his

hands firmly in his pockets as he returned to his desk. He hated the feelings churning in his gut, making him do and say things that would make the turmoil inside him visible.

'Okay,' she said softly, still standing in the doorway. 'Mrs Williams told me you're leaving for Zafar at noon tomorrow. If I don't get to see you, I hope… I hope everything goes well.'

His head jerked round, the vicious twist of longing making the hollow ache drop into his stomach. And suddenly he knew he wasn't ready to let her go.

'You need not worry about seeing me tomorrow,' he said. 'As you shall be accompanying me to Zafar.'

'I… I don't understand.' Orla was so shocked by Karim's bold statement she stuttered over the words.

She'd been standing in the doorway to his office watching him, for several minutes, before alerting him to her presence. He'd looked shattered. His shoulders bowed, his dark hair dishevelled, his eyes staring at the papers in his hand but clearly not reading them.

He had seemed so different from the harsh, indomitable man she had come to know, her heart had pulsed painfully in her chest.

She had no right to care about him, or what

he was going through. But he'd looked so different too, from the vital, playful man who had whipped her senses into a frenzy the day before, that she hadn't been able to control the wave of sympathy.

He'd been locked in his office ever since learning of his father's death with a series of assistants and delegates, diplomats and executives. This was the first moment she'd been able to get him alone... Had he even slept since getting the news yesterday? The bruised shadows under his eyes made it seem unlikely.

'I didn't think you'd need me any more,' she blurted out when he didn't say anything, just pinned her with that intense glare that made her nerve-endings sizzle and spark.

Although she'd been told nothing about her situation, she'd assumed she would be returning to Kildare. Now his father was dead, why would he need a fake fiancée?

'Did you read the engagement contract you signed?' he said, his voice gruff.

'Yes, but...' The truth was she hadn't read the contract's every detail, but she knew what it contained.

'Then you know the Ruling Council are expecting me to travel to Zafar with my future Queen. Breaking off the engagement so soon after my father's death is a disruption the country can do without while it is already facing a constitutional crisis.' He paused, and she could sense his frustration. But then his gaze met hers, and the stark challenge in his eyes made heat flush into her cheeks. 'And I think we both know there is unfinished business between us.'

She nodded, trying to ignore the bubble of something building under her breastbone.

She'd been prepared for him to discard her, had been ready to leave his home tomorrow, perhaps never to see him again. But the truth was, her reaction to that possibility hadn't been nearly as simple or straightforward as it should have been. She had tried to convince herself that was because he had introduced her to a world of physical pleasure she hadn't even known existed. But as she stared back at him now, his eyes shadowed with fatigue and frustration and a grief he refused to acknowledge, she knew her reluctance to leave him was about more than just the physical connection they shared.

'Okay, if you're sure you need me,' she said. 'I'll make sure I'm ready.'

The bubble under her breastbone turned into something that felt suspiciously like tenderness when she watched the rigid line of his shoulders soften.

Had he been expecting her to argue? To refuse to honour the terms of their agreement?

Perhaps she should have. After all, there had been no mention of her travelling all the way to Zafar. And a part of her had wanted to return to Kildare, where everything was so much more simple and straightforward.

But they both knew this wasn't just about maintaining their charade any more. Or avoiding making the constitutional crisis of his father's death any worse.

He was right, there was unfinished business between them. And she wanted to finish it.

'I'll have Jason give you all the details first thing in the morning,' he said, picking up the papers again. 'Get a good night's sleep. It's a long journey through the desert to the Palace of Kings.'

'Will do,' she murmured, then added impulsively, 'Perhaps you should do the same. You look exhausted.'

He stared at her for a long moment and she wondered if she'd overstepped the mark. After all, his welfare wasn't really supposed to be her concern. But then his lips quirked in a rueful smile. 'Point taken,' he said.

But as she turned to leave, stupidly pleased by the oddly domestic moment, he added, 'By the way, Orla. Don't worry, I won't expect you to actually marry me once we're there.'

She paused and turned back. The smile had

disappeared, and the intense stare had returned, almost as if he was trying to gauge her reaction. She forced herself to stifle the tiny flicker of disappointment, knowing it had nothing to do with the thought of not marrying him, but rather the sudden loss of that precious moment of camaraderie.

Was he concerned that she was getting the wrong idea? That by agreeing to go with him without complaint, she was expecting more? She forced a smile to her lips and said, 'That's a relief. As I'm sure I'd make a disastrous queen.'

He choked out a rough chuckle and the odd sense of elation returned as the tension eased. 'I doubt you'd make a worse queen than I will make a king,' he said.

She knew that wasn't true. She'd seen how hard he had been working already and how seriously he took his responsibility, to do the right thing, for his country and his people—even though he had professed a week ago to have no loyalty to either. And she couldn't think of a man who was more confident or decisive, who wielded such an air of command or authority the way he did—all of which surely made him the perfect candidate to lead any country out of a constitutional crisis.

But she could see the weary cynicism in his eyes, and had heard the bitter edge in his tone…

And she doubted anything she had to say on the subject would convince him, so she simply smiled and decided to lighten the mood instead.

'Whatever you say, Your Majesty. I'll see you at noon tomorrow. If nothing else this should be a grand adventure,' she finished, pleased when she heard another tired chuckle.

'Yeah, right,' he murmured.

When she got back to her suite, she sent Dervla a text, telling her she was heading to Zafar, then switched off her phone.

She did not need to be bombarded with a ton of fanciful nonsense by her sister right now.

But as she put the phone down and got ready for bed, the bubble of exhilaration she hadn't really acknowledged until this moment expanded.

Going to Zafar with Karim *would* be a grand adventure. So much about Karim fascinated and excited her.

Here was a chance to discover more about him, and to see where this *thing*, this connection, or whatever it was between them, might lead. She would be well outside her comfort zone again, but was that really a bad thing? She'd spent so many years making a place for herself—finding a purpose—in Kildare, in some ways her work there had become a prison. She'd become scared to try anything new, to move away from the comfortable, the familiar and take a chance. She'd allowed her weaknesses as well as her strengths to define her, but Karim had already shown he had confidence in her abilities. Now she just needed to be brave again. And bold. And see where this new adventure might lead her.

She sobered, recalling the flash of confusion, even vulnerability on Karim's face when he'd lifted his head earlier to find her standing in the doorway of his study.

The death of his father had hurt Karim in ways she was fairly sure he wasn't even aware of.

He needed her support. Even if he refused to admit it. Because however short, or fake, or fleeting their relationship, she understood what he was going through because she'd been through it herself when her own father had died a year ago. She'd had to pick herself up, deal with the conflicting emotions she felt towards a man she'd once loved and looked up to who had let her and her sister down terribly in the end. Coping with her grief in the midst of all that had been next to impossible—and the only way she'd survived it was by immersing herself in work, in caring for the horses she loved, and by leaning on Dervla and Maeve and Gerry and her other friends and colleagues.

Karim had more than enough work to keep

him busy, but he didn't seem to have any friends, anyone who could lift his spirits or look out for him when the going got really tough.

And maybe she wasn't his friend—and he didn't want her support—but he had rescued her once. Was it really so wrong to want to rescue him in return?

CHAPTER TEN

AS THE CHAUFFEUR-DRIVEN cavalcade of vehicles crested the rocky terrain and the minarets of Zafar's Palace of the Kings sparkled in the setting sun in the distance, the dark thoughts that had defined so much of Karim's boyhood and adolescence crowded into his mind.

His mother's pale, drawn face—which looked so young now from the distance of twenty-two years. The tight thin line of his father's lips, the spark of anger in his golden eyes—signals that Karim had displeased him again and would be punished.

Karim tensed, humiliated by the dropping sensation in his stomach—the echo of that long-ago fear—as the car rolled through the palace gates, and made its way past the honour guard of tribesmen and uniformed officers in Zafar's red and gold livery.

A soft gasp beside him yanked him free from the bitter memories. And he turned to see Orla, her vibrant hair contrasting with her pale skin as she stared in awe at the palace's golden walls. They passed into the lavish inner sanctum of lush planting, exotic birds and trees, elaborate fountains and deep pools of blue-green water created in defiant contrast to the barren desert that surrounded them.

'It's so beautiful,' she remarked, those wide emerald eyes meeting his.

'Is it?' he said as the familiar spike of desire and yearning—and something more debilitating, an emotion he couldn't and wouldn't name—accosted him. He quashed it, as he had so many times in the last ten hours, ever since he'd met her on the heliport in Belgravia.

Just knowing she was with him, tucked in a seat at the back of the private jet reading a book, had helped to calm him down while he worked with his advisors during the long plane journey. But being in this damn car with her for two hours, for the drive from Zafar's main airport, had been nothing short of torture. The phantom sound of soft sobs, the very real scent of her permeating his senses, had put his whole body on high alert while he was supposed to be concentrating on how the hell to navigate the next few days, weeks, God help him, probably even months…

She'd caught him at a weak moment the night

before, and he'd given in to the need coursing through his body—to have her by his side while he dealt with this new reality. But it wasn't just the familiar surge of heat that accosted him as she stared back at him, her eyes seeing so much more than he wanted her to see. Just as they had last night.

'I'm sorry you don't think so,' she said.

The intuitive remark made the vice around his ribs—which had dogged him ever since he'd learned of his father's death—tighten.

Why had he really wanted her here? Was it just to finally satisfy the sweaty erotic dreams that had pursued him for days now? Or the expediency of not creating a diplomatic incident by terminating the engagement too soon…? Or was it more than that?

Why had he been incapable of leaving her behind, when he'd never had a problem facing his demons alone before now?

One thing was for sure. He would have her tonight—and put at least one damn demon to rest.

'Once the official introductions are concluded, I'll have you escorted to my quarters,' he said, the tightness in his chest joined by the much more familiar spike of desire.

The blush hit her cheeks. 'Okay,' she said softly.

The breath he hadn't even realised he was

holding gushed out at the indication that she was still willing.

Perhaps he hadn't been wrong to bring her with him. His motives didn't have to be that complicated. It *would* have been hard to explain her absence to the Ruling Council. And Orla, with her wide eyes, wild hair, lush lips and glorious body, had always been an excellent distraction. Perhaps she was smarter and funnier and more engaging than he had realised, her wry wit and willingness to challenge him a turn-on he hadn't expected. But he was going to need some light relief over the next few days, maybe even weeks, and Orla seemed the ideal person to supply it—in so many ways.

'I have no doubt the Ruling Council will have lined up a series of tedious meetings and briefings which I will be unable to escape today,' he said.

He lifted her hand, allowing himself to touch her for the first time since their escapade two long days ago in the car journey back from Hammonds. She jerked, as he brought her fingers to his lips and kissed the knuckles. A rueful smile tilted his lips as he released her and registered her heightened breathing. Good to know he wasn't the only one being tortured by the enforced celibacy of the last few days. 'But

I'll join you as soon as I can,' he finished, unable to disguise the husky promise in his voice.

She nodded, her cheeks now a beguiling shade of scarlet.

He had to bite his tongue, to contain the rough chuckle of satisfaction that wanted to burst out of his mouth.

Damn but he wanted her. So much. Surely satisfying this driving hunger would simplify his feelings for her? Feelings that had become unnecessarily complicated, just like every other thing in his life right now.

'The madness should settle down in a couple of days,' he added, or maybe in a couple of weeks. 'Then we can discuss your future.'

After this much anticipation, he doubted either one of them would be satisfied too quickly. He wanted to explore every inch of her fragrant flesh, to see her lose herself again, but this time while he was embedded inside the tight wet warmth of... He dragged his mind away from the thoughts that had been crucifying him for days.

Not helping, Karim. Not when you have several hours ahead of you of tedious bureaucracy before you can finally make her yours.

He cleared the blockage in his throat. 'I expect you'll want to return to Kildare?' he said, trying to keep the conversation on practicalities to drown the heat.

Something flickered across her face that looked oddly like disappointment. He dismissed it, along with the idiotic leap in his chest. They'd already agreed that this was a temporary arrangement, which suited them both.

'Yes,' she said.

He nodded, glad when the car finally cruised to a stop, in front of the dramatic Moorish structure that towered above them like a glowering giant.

A row of dignitaries and diplomats, including the delegation who had turned up in London two days ago, stood in their ceremonial robes waiting to greet him.

One of the palace servants rushed forward to open the door.

The traditional wailing cries of the local tribesmen, punctuated by the ceremonial cannon fire from outside the palace walls to celebrate the arrival of the new King, became deafening as he struggled to ignore the provocative promise in Orla's eyes and step out of the car.

She joined him a few moments later. He had to place his hand on her hip, far too aware of her tremble of response and the effect it had on him, as he guided her through the introductions to a never-ending line of dignitaries.

As they finally neared the end, and approached the line of palace staff, he knew he'd had enough. The journey had been tiring for them both, and, even though he'd managed to get some much-needed sleep last night, having her so close was taxing his resolve, not to mention the last remaining reserves of his patience. He needed to get Orla safely ensconced in his rooms, if he were to have any hope of surviving the next few hours without sporting an erection the size of the tower above them.

Drawing the introductions to a halt, he called over the man whom they'd already been introduced to as his father's former head of household.

'Um… Saed,' he said, glad he'd managed to remember the man's name as he pressed his hand to Orla's hip. Now he'd begun touching her it was becoming harder and harder to stop. 'Could you take my fiancée to my chambers?' Apart from anything else, he wanted Orla well rested, because he planned to keep her very busy tonight. 'And make sure she has everything she needs.'

The older man's brows shot up his forehead, his expression a picture of shock, his skin darkening as he flushed. 'But, Your Majesty, it will bring much dishonour on yourself and Mistress Calhoun for such an arrangement before the wedding on Friday.'

'The... *What* wedding?' he snapped. Orla stiffened beside him, obviously as horrified as he was by this information. 'I didn't authorise a wedding,' he said, his voice raw with fury.

What the hell was going on? He'd never been informed of any such arrangement. Certainly hadn't sanctioned it.

'The Ruling Council made arrangements for your convenience, Your Majesty,' the man said, his eyes darting towards the council members who were standing on the other side of the courtyard, out of earshot.

'What...?' Karim bit off the swear word as the man flinched. 'What convenience?'

This was intolerable, inconceivable. He had never given any indication he wished for a wedding to be arranged on his behalf.

He could feel Orla beside him, trembling. Did she think he had engineered this, lured her here to trap her into marriage?

The fury was tempered by the brutal stab of guilt... And the hazy pain of memory. His mother's face dragged him back to the darkest days of his childhood, the words she had uttered so many times in her distress, before she took her own life.

He didn't love me, Karim. He used me, he tricked me, and then he discarded me, because he never really wanted me.

Other memories, ones he'd blocked for so long, clawed at the edges of his consciousness as Saed continued talking.

'For Your Majesty's convenience,' the man said, his face getting redder as his confusion and concern increased at Karim's reaction. 'The Ruling Council believed…' He trailed off, his gaze darting to Orla, who had gone painfully still beside him.

Why did that only make this worse? That she hadn't asked him to explain? What did she think was happening here?

'What did they believe?' he snapped through gritted teeth, trying to control his temper, and the bitter pulse of guilt.

'It was always your father's way, to arrange a wedding as soon as possible so that…' Saed trailed off again.

His father? The mention of the man he had always despised had the fury galloping into his throat. The bastard had tried to manipulate him in life and now he was managing to do it from beyond the grave? He wasn't going to tolerate this.

'So that *what*?' he demanded, his voice rising, but he suspected he already knew the answer.

'So that he wouldn't have to wait,' the man replied so softly Karim could barely hear him. 'To consummate the marriage.'

Of course.

His father had enjoyed exploiting women. He had used them and discarded them. Sometimes he married then, sometimes he didn't, but when he wanted a woman one thing he never did was wait.

'The Ruling Council have arranged for Mistress Calhoun to be housed in the Women's Quarters, as is tradition, to honour her as your betrothed, until the marriage is performed,' Saed continued, practically quaking now.

Karim felt sick—as the implications of what had happened began to sink in—and shame engulfed him. This catastrophe wasn't Saed's fault. Any more than it was the fault of the Ruling Council. They had simply assumed he was as much of an entitled, insatiable bastard where women were concerned as his father—and they had been trying to honour Orla as his betrothed while also giving him what they had assumed he would demand, this woman in his bed as soon as possible.

The irony—that he had brought Orla to Zafar intending to do exactly that without actually marrying her—only made this situation more screwed up.

But the truth was, the only person to blame for this catastrophe, other than a dead man, was himself.

'It's okay, Karim. I can go to the Women's Quarters now, if that works best for everyone.'

At the quietly spoken words, he turned to Orla. But where he had been prepared to see accusation and disgust, maybe even fear, all he saw was concern… And something far worse—trust.

Why did that only make him feel like more of a bastard?

What had he ever really done to deserve her trust? How could she have so much faith in him and his motives, when he had done nothing to earn it?

The look in her eyes reminded him for one agonising moment of the woman who had clung to him, after he had marched across a ballroom to protect her from the unwanted advances of another man. In that moment, as her fingers gripped his neck and her face pressed into his shirt, she had seemed more like a girl than a woman. An innocent, vulnerable girl who deserved to be cherished and had needed his protection.

The pulse of guilt and shame threatened to engulf him again at the disturbing thought that the man she needed protecting from now was him.

'That would probably be for the best, until I can get this sorted out,' he said, his voice so rough it scraped against his throat like sandpaper.

'I will have Mistress Calhoun escorted to the Women's Quarters immediately,' Saed announced, clicking his fingers to summon two women over from the line of palace staff. The manservant looked so relieved at this new turn of events, it was almost funny.

Although Karim had never felt less like laughing.

If he'd been angry at the prospect of being forced to take his father's place on the throne of Zafar, now he felt sickened by his own actions.

He'd always believed he was a much better man than the man who had sired him. Had always taken his moral superiority for granted, but when had it ever really been tested until now? And already he'd been found wanting.

He'd brought Orla with him to Zafar because it had been the expedient thing to do politically, but also because he had wanted her for himself. He had convinced himself his sexual needs took precedence over everything else—and had quite possibly put her into an untenable position as a result. Because getting this wedding stopped now might well be impossible.

How the hell was he going to explain to the Ruling Council he did not wish the wedding to go ahead as planned without also cluing them into the fact the engagement had simply been a ruse to frustrate his father? Whatever he did now, he realised, with a bitter sense of regret, Orla and he would not be able to feed the hunger tonight.

How could he have her brought to his chambers without raising lots of questions about his own integrity, not to mention the integrity of their engagement?

He tried to remain as dispassionate as possible while Saed introduced Orla to the two women who were about to take her away from him, for God only knew how long. One was an older woman called Ameera, who was Orla's most senior lady-in-waiting, while the younger woman, Jamilla, had been hired as the new Queen's PA.

As the older woman fussed over Orla, Karim was finally forced to lift his hand from her hip. Before she could leave him though, he snagged her wrist and tugged her round to face him. Tucking a knuckle under her chin, he lifted her face to his.

'Don't panic, Orla,' he murmured, so only she could hear him, before he placed a parting kiss on her lips. He'd compromised both of them enough already by reacting so violently to Saed's mention of the wedding. He needed to calm down and work out a solution. 'I'll figure this out.'

He forced himself to draw back and let her go. Perhaps having her safely ensconced in the Women's Quarters wasn't such a bad thing. At least it ought to stop him thinking with a part of his anatomy that wasn't his brain. Something he'd been doing way too much of recently.

To his surprise, given how badly he'd messed up, instead of looking anxious or annoyed, she sent him another uncomplicated, far too trusting smile—the shadow of desire in her eyes undimmed. 'It's grand, Karim. I'm not panicking. I have faith in you.'

But as he watched her walk away, the sway of her hips doing nothing to dim the hunger that had got them both into this fix in the first place, he realised it wasn't her faith in him that was the problem.

It was his faith in himself.

He'd strived his whole life not to be a man like his father. Had always been sure to be honest and open in his relationships with women. To let them know what he could offer and what he could not. But with Orla, nothing had ever been that easy or uncomplicated. And now he'd crossed a line he wasn't sure he had the strength, or the integrity, to uncross.

CHAPTER ELEVEN

'YOUR HAIR IS like flame, Orla. Is it real, or from a bottle?'

'It's real.' Orla choked out a strained laugh at the typically forthright comment from Ameera, as the older woman washed her hair. Thank goodness for Ameera's chatty, friendly presence or she would probably have lost her mind completely in the last two days.

She'd been in Zafar for nearly seventy-two hours now, most of it cocooned in the palace's lavish women's quarters.

The morning after she'd arrived she'd been given a tour of the stables by Karim's stable manager, who had told her the new King wanted her advice on the care of the beautiful Arabian stallions that had once belonged to his father. She'd been flattered by Karim's faith in her, and at least it had given her something to do, but she'd also been disappointed that she hadn't had a chance to see him herself. So far the only contact she'd had with Karim personally was a two-line note yesterday morning, thanking her for her feedback on the horses, which he had said was invaluable, and then a cryptic mention of how he was working on 'resolving their situation to everyone's satisfaction'.

But since then she'd heard nothing—and the wedding was tonight. Ameera, though, and the other ladies-in-waiting, seemed convinced it was going ahead—in approximately four hours' time—because they had arrived in her suite of rooms that morning and insisted on beginning the seemingly endless process of preparing her to become the new Queen of Zafar.

Orla had never felt more embarrassed or confused or anxious in her life.

But she'd had no choice but to try and force herself to relax.

Whatever was going on diplomatically, she hadn't lied to Karim, she trusted him. He'd sounded as shocked as she had felt when Saed had informed him of the planned event, and she had no doubt he had probably been trying to prevent it from happening. But it had dawned on her this morning, when Ameera and the other women had begun gossiping, brimming with excitement at the prospect of the wedding—and all the guests who had begun to arrive—that getting it stopped might have turned out to be an impossible feat. Not least because how was Karim going to do that without admitting to everyone theirs was not a real engagement?

It was a humongous mess, she could see that, and possibly not one he was best placed to deal with when his whole life had already been thrown into turmoil by the huge challenges the country faced in the wake of his father's death—something that had also been a hot topic of discussion among the women.

'You are very tense,' Ameera said, massaging Orla's scalp with a fragrant shampoo scented with bergamot and orange. 'You must not be nervous. The wedding will be a glorious event. The whole of Zafar is excited to greet our new Queen as well as our new King.'

Orla swallowed down the hysterical laugh that had been threatening to pop out of her mouth all morning at Ameera's generous words—the flush of guilt, though, was impossible to contain.

What would Ameera and the rest of Zafar's population think if they knew she and Karim hardly knew each other? And that this whole engagement was a total fraud?

The flush intensified, though, as she remembered Karim's bold kiss when they had parted and the fierce possessiveness in his gaze as she'd been led away.

Okay, maybe they weren't a *total* fraud any more. She cared about him, and what he was going through. Probably more than she should. And she still wanted him, desperately. As the minutes had ticked by over the last forty-eight hours and she'd got no more word from him about whether the wedding had been cancelled, she'd come to the conclusion that maybe going through with it wouldn't be so terrible. Especially if it meant they could finally deal with the driving hunger that had consumed them both— well, certainly her anyway—for days now.

After all, if they could fake an engagement, why couldn't they fake a marriage?

'You blush very prettily,' Ameera said, grinning, as she finished rinsing Orla's hair.

Orla felt the blush ignite. *Terrific.* As if this situation weren't awkward enough, now everyone could see how eager she was to end up in Karim's bed.

Way to go, Orla, it's official, you're a total hussy.

'The new King is very handsome…' Ameera murmured, the indulgent smile in her voice only making Orla feel more exposed. But then the woman added, 'From the way he kissed you in the courtyard, so tender and so much in love, I think he is not a man like his father—and you are nothing like his mother—so your wedding night should be a good one.'

Ameera laughed as she draped a linen cloth over Orla's head to dry her hair.

Orla straightened in her chair and turned to meet Ameera's gaze, surprised by the mention of Karim's parents.

She had been in the quarters for three days now, and she'd got the definite impression no one wanted to talk about the dead King. Because every time his name was mentioned in front of her, looks were exchanged and the subject was changed. Which, now she thought about it, was beyond weird. After all, he had died less than a week ago.

All she knew about Karim's mother were the things she'd discovered while trawling the Internet for information about him the day before she had met him. By reading old press reports, she had discovered that Cassandra Wainwright had been a young British heiress, who had married and divorced King Abdullah, returned to England with her son and then died five years later when Karim was still only ten years old... Which was perhaps why he had never mentioned her. But why was there so little information about her? Orla had been able to find virtually nothing out about the death of the former Queen of Zafar, or why the marriage had ended.

Until Ameera's cryptic comment.

'I think he is not a man like his father—and you are nothing like his mother—so your wedding night should be a good one.'

She probably shouldn't ask Ameera about Karim's parents. His past was none of her business. But she was desperately curious about them both. She knew Karim hadn't had a good relationship with his father, but she also knew how much he was struggling with his death, even if he didn't want to admit it. And now she was wondering about what had happened to his mother on her wedding night, too.

Was being curious about Karim's parents and their relationship so wrong? After all, she might well have to actually marry Karim this evening, because they were running out of time to have the wedding stopped.

'Did you know Karim's mother, Ameera?' Orla blurted out.

Ameera's smile faltered, and her eyes lost the twinkle of amusement that had been an essential part of her personality over the last few days. Did she regret letting the information slip? Orla felt sure she did, but just when she was convinced Ameera would refuse to answer, the lady-in-waiting nodded. 'Yes, I knew the King's second wife. I was a maid in the palace, when she first arrived here and they married.'

'What was she like?' Orla asked.

'The King has not spoken of his mother to you?' the woman asked, her gaze kind, but also probing.

Orla blushed at the perceptive comment, but the lady-in-waiting's gaze remained kind and knowing.

'Karim and I haven't known each other that long,' Orla said, carefully. That definitely wasn't a lie. 'He's never talked to me about his mother, but I know he didn't get on very well with his father.'

Ameera let out a sad laugh. 'The new King has not visited Zafar since he was a boy, and has not seen his father in over a decade, so, yes, it is true. They did not get on well.' The sad smile flattened to be replaced with a guarded expression. 'I am afraid I cannot tell you about what went on in the marriage, because Cassandra swore me to secrecy many years ago. And it is a vow I have never broken. His Majesty was only five when he left Zafar with his mother, but I think if he was aware...' She paused, sighed. 'Then he would not wish me to speak of it either.'

Orla's pulse pounded heavily at Ameera's statement—and the sadness in her eyes, which was so unlike her usually cheerful demeanour.

So something had been terribly wrong in the marriage before the divorce, and Karim might have witnessed it? Was that where the haunted look had come from when they drove through the walls of the palace into the grounds?

He'd insisted he had no feelings for his father, but it had been obvious then, as well as the night she had gone to his study, that the truth was more complex. Perhaps it wasn't that he didn't have feelings for his father, but that he didn't want to have feelings for him.

'Do you…? Do you know why Karim and his father didn't get along?' she asked.

He had seemed so alone in his study that night, but also during the flight over and the journey to the palace. So closed off and wary and tense. Karim had always been dominant, commanding, pragmatic rather than demonstrative, so it hadn't really surprised her that he hadn't wanted to lean on anyone, let alone her. But she knew he could also be playful, and unbelievably hot—because she'd glimpsed that man too during the heated moments they'd shared in the car—before all this had happened.

And she wanted to help him find that man again. Somehow.

But how could she do that, when she had no idea what he was struggling with? She knew he needed a friend, but how could she be a good friend if she didn't know more about where that haunted look came from?

'All I can tell you,' Ameera began, 'although you must not repeat this to anyone, for it is disrespectful to talk so of a king…'

Orla nodded, realising that Ameera was taking a risk by speaking to her so candidly about her former employer.

'Is that King Abdullah, His Majesty's father, was not a man made for marriage…' Ameera paused as if looking for the right words. 'Or, I think, for fatherhood. He could be harsh, as a husband. And also as a father. During the summers His Majesty Karim came back here to Zafar as part of the divorce settlement, they clashed often—especially as His Majesty got older—and the old King would have him punished severely for his disrespect.'

'Oh, no.' Orla felt her throat closing. Poor Karim, no wonder he was so conflicted now about assuming the throne. And still so angry with his father.

Although her relationship with her own father had become increasingly difficult after her mother's death, he'd never been a violent man, or a cruel one, or not intentionally so—just increasingly absent.

She was getting the impression King Abdullah Zakar Amari Khan had been both.

'It must be such a struggle for him to assume the throne if that's his only role model,' she murmured.

'The new King's advisors say he is very competent and has already made many good changes that are long overdue,' Ameera interrupted Orla's thoughts.

Orla's heart stuttered at the odd wave of pride.

She could well imagine Karim would make a good monarch, he certainly made an extremely efficient businessman, although it wasn't really what she'd meant.

As if guessing as much though, Ameera added, 'But his manservant tells me he does not sleep well at night. That he wakes from nightmares and paces his chamber. They believe he is troubled, yes, but it is not their place to understand what is in His Majesty's heart,' she finished and Orla heard the soft note of censure.

No, it wasn't the place of Karim's advisors or servants to understand what was in his heart—nor could they help him wrestle his demons, whatever they were—because that wasn't a job of an employee, it was a job of the woman he loved.

And okay, maybe she wasn't actually that woman. But she was all he had at the moment.

Over the last seventy-two hours she'd been panicking about her own situation. Worrying about what it would mean if she and Karim were forced to go through with this wedding.

But she could see clearly now that Karim was the one who needed an anchor—even more than she did right now. Perhaps it was time to show Karim she could help out with more than just his father's Arabian stallions.

'I need to see the King now,' she said.

Ameera frowned. 'That is not good luck for your marriage, to see him so soon before the wedding.'

Right. So they had the same silly superstitions in Zafar as they did in Kildare. She sighed. 'How about if I wrote a note?' she asked. 'Could someone deliver it?'

'That would be very romantic.' Ameera smiled, obviously pleased with the idea of her and Karim sending each other love notes. 'I can deliver it, while the ladies prepare your bath.'

'Grand,' Orla said.

Now all she had to do was figure out what to write, so Karim would know she was ready to go along with the wedding if that was what he needed. And she was here for him, if that was what he needed, too.

'Sheikh Zane and Queen Catherine of Narabia and Prince Kasim and Princess Kasia of the Kholadi tribal lands have just arrived at the palace with their entourages. Would you like me to have them taken to their rooms before you greet them?'

Karim glared at Saed Khouri, his head of household, and tried not to snap at the man—especially when the older man flinched and bowed deeply.

Perhaps it was time he admitted defeat. He'd been in negotiations with the Ruling Council for three days now, trying to be diplomatic as he arranged to postpone or cancel this damn wedding while also dealing with a million and one other issues—some large, some small, all urgent—and he'd got absolutely nowhere. While carrying out all his other orders and decrees, the council had effectively steamrollered over all his suggestions to do with the wedding, and now apparently they hadn't even got around to cancelling the invitations to the neighbouring rulers and other VIP guests that had been sent without his permission.

No way was he going to be able to stop the wedding now.

'Sure, you do that, Saed,' he said, not making much of an effort to hide his frustration. 'I'll greet them properly in an hour,' he said, distracted by the thought of the conversation he was going to have to have now with Orla.

'Make sure they have everything they need in the meantime.'

Karim had met Zane Khan, a distant cousin, and his British wife, Catherine, a few times at events in London and New York and he'd had a few business dealings with Zane's half-brother, Raif, aka Prince Kasim, but knowing both men and their wives and children had been invited to witness this fake event was not improving his temper.

Karim's frontal lobe started to pulse as Saed left his study.

Somehow or other he was going to have to explain this whole mess to Orla, and ask her to go through with the wedding. Perhaps he could offer her the job she'd asked for at Calhouns, or something similar. And include the payment she'd originally turned down? A million euros would surely sweeten the prospect of having to pretend to be his Queen for any length of time. But even as he contemplated doing that, he felt the bitter taste in his mouth. How could he offer her money? When he still planned to have a wedding night with her? It was the only damn thing that made the thought of going through with this farce tolerable. Wouldn't offering her money now be like paying her for sex? Of course, he'd had mistresses in the past, who he had supported financially... But his situation with Orla was not the same. Something about her had always been different from the other women he'd dated. He would certainly never have contemplated going through a marriage ceremony with any of them. Would never have trusted them not to take advantage of the situation. But strangely he did trust Orla. And he wasn't even sure why.

Maybe it was that moment when she had told him she trusted him? Or maybe it had happened before that, perhaps when she had responded with such artless abandon in his arms in the car journey from Hammonds? Or was it that first night, when she had clung to him and looked to him for protection? And for one terrifying moment, all he'd wanted to do was keep her safe.

It would be deeply ironic—that a woman he was being forced to marry had come to mean more to him than any other woman before her— if it weren't so damn disturbing. How did you tell someone you actually respected, and who you cared enough about not to use, that you were going to have to use them anyway? He had no idea, as he'd never allowed anyone to get so close to him before. And now he was going to be forced—thanks to what he was sure was the deliberate intransigence of his Ruling Council—to let Orla get closer still.

Karim paced the length of the ornate room,

and finally let go of the curse word that had been building inside him.

He had forced himself not to see Orla again before he could give her a definitive answer about the wedding. But he wasn't sure going to her now was a good idea. After the agony of spending eight hours in a plane with her and two hours in a car—on the journey here—and not being able to put his hands on her, perhaps they both deserved the chance to savour the moment, to spend a long, indulgent night together once this farce was done with?

The knock on the door of his chambers dragged his attention back to the present, but did nothing to stem the hot pulse of heat that tormented him whenever he thought of her.

'Who is it?' he shouted out.

'Your Majesty, it is Hakim,' his young man-servant called out. 'I have a message for you delivered by Ameera, your fiancée's lady-in-waiting.'

Karim frowned. This had to be from Orla, demanding to know what the hell was going on. And how could he blame her? 'Bring it in.'

The young man came in and bowed, then handed him a handwritten note. He recognised Orla's swirling handwriting on the envelope, even though he'd only seen it once—when she had signed their engagement contract.

How had so much changed, in so short a time?

The ache in his crotch throbbed as he took the envelope off the silver salver and caught a lungful of her scent, which clung to the paper. He ripped open the envelope. He read the message and felt the vice around his ribs squeeze.

Karim,

I know you're super-busy at the moment, but I just wanted to tell you however you need to handle our 'situation' today, I'm good with it.

BTW, I'm also a great listener. I know ours is not a conventional engagement, but sometimes grief can surprise us and we need a friend.

Orla x

Karim stared at the note. The simple compassion in the words made the hollow ache that had dogged him ever since he had learned of his father's sudden death turn into a gaping hole in the pit of his stomach.

How did Orla know that he needed her?

He tensed—suddenly feeling more transparent, more vulnerable than he had since he was a boy. And he'd sat in the cold church, staring at the wicket casket covered in flowers, the heavy perfume of the late summer blooms masking the musty smell of old hymnals, his legs dangling from the pew, as tears stung his eyes and he tried to figure out why his mother had left him, when he'd tried so hard to make her happy.

'Your Majesty, do you have a reply I can give Ameera?'

He looked up to find the young man watching him expectantly. The brutal heat flared into his cheeks as he recognised the hollow ache for what it was. A weakness he could not afford to indulge. And could not allow anyone to see.

He crushed the note in his fist. Leaning on Orla was not an option.

He shouldn't want her care or her compassion. He couldn't accept it. Because it would turn him into that defenceless child again—frightened and alone.

'Yes,' he said, the grim determination in his words not helping to fill the hole in his stomach. Returning to his desk, he jotted down a note on a piece of paper and folded it, sealed it in an envelope and handed it to the servant.

'Tell Ameera to give this to Miss Calhoun.'

As Hakim nodded and left, Karim picked up the phone and asked to have his call connected to Carstairs in London.

He needed to arrange to have Orla returned to Kildare as soon as possible after the ceremony. He could then have the marriage annulled discreetly in a few months' time. There would be questions at first about the Queen's absence, but his course was clear. He was being forced to go through with this ceremony, but that was all he could go through with. He couldn't risk making this relationship any more real than it already was. She'd slipped under his guard somehow. And he had to minimise the damage.

She had come to mean too much to him.

Perhaps it was just sexual frustration, the rare chemistry that he had struggled to control, the strange circumstances of their situation, or simply the stress of being forced to assume a legacy he had always believed he would be able to avoid—and the nightmares that had assailed him ever since his return to his father's home. But whatever the reason, Orla was not the solution to controlling emotions he had thought dead and buried a lifetime ago.

He explained the situation to Carstairs and listened to the man's stunned surprise at his decision to end his contract with Orla—'Damn, that's a shame, Karim, you two looked so good together.'

But the hollow ache, and the inconvenient heat, refused to subside, convincing him that tonight was going to be the longest, most agonising night of his life.

CHAPTER TWELVE

'You look beautiful, Orla,' Ameera murmured as she rolled the veil over Orla's face.

Orla breathed out a nervous sigh, far too aware of the butterflies going berserk in her stomach as the sound of the waiting guests and dignitaries could be heard in the courtyard beyond. Night had fallen a few minutes before, casting a golden glow over the large antechamber where she had spent several hours being dressed and primped and perfumed and styled to within an inch of her life by a small army of hair and make-up professionals.

'Thanks, Ameera,' she said, catching a glimpse of herself in the silver standing mirror near the door.

Her gaze stared through the veil at the stunning red and gold silk dress embroidered with a thousand tiny gems that draped over her figure like a whisper, to reveal the fitted bodice and skirt beneath of traditional Zafari royal wedding attire. Her usually mad hair had somehow been tamed into a cascade of curls, while her eyes had been made up with black kohl to look huge. The make-up artist might as well not have bothered, because her eyes widened to the size of saucers all on their own when she heard the crowd being quietened in the courtyard beyond. A crowd packed with kings and queens, princes and princesses, heads of state and dignitaries from Zafar and its neighbouring countries—all people she didn't know, and who didn't know her.

She could hear the announcement of the wedding being made in Zafari and then English by the man who had come to speak to her in detail about the ceremony a few hours ago—right after Karim's note had arrived, the contents of which continued to whirl round and round in her head.

Orla,

I'm afraid we will have to go through with this farce of a wedding, but I have already made arrangements for your return to Kildare.

In the circumstances, I think it best we don't share a chamber after the ceremony, so that we may obtain an annulment quickly.

K

The butterflies turned into dive-bombers in her stomach as she forced herself to draw several steadying breaths and ignore the foolish well of disappointment and sadness.

Why was she getting so freaked out?

He hadn't rejected her, he'd simply stated how things would have to proceed.

But why then couldn't she get rid of the sharp stab of inadequacy?

Ameera finished adjusting the veil, as the wedding music began and the dive-bombing butterflies threatened to explode out of the top of her head.

'It is time, Your Highness,' Ameera squeezed her hand. 'Do not fear, you will make His Majesty a wonderful bride.'

Except he doesn't want me as a bride, or anything else.

'Thank you, Ameera,' she said, gripping her friend's fingers back.

The huge brass-panelled doors to the room opened and she was forced to let Ameera go.

Clasping her hands together, she stepped out into the courtyard, flanked by the Queen's honour guard—who were dressed in long red robes embroidered with gold thread.

Just keep going. And don't trip.

She forced her feet to move in the red silk slippers along a path lit by torchlight and strewn with rose blossoms leading into the palace's central garden. She could see faces, so many faces staring back at her. She tried to take some of them in to calm down the dive-bombing butterflies and the pain in her stomach.

A striking man dressed in black tribal wear cradling a beautiful toddler in his arms bowed his head as she passed, while his equally stunning and heavily pregnant wife, who held an identical toddler's hand, curtsied and sent her a sunny smile.

That smile helped to get Orla past the next line of lavishly dressed diplomats and dignitaries, their critical gaze making her certain they must be able to see what a fraud she was. Then she passed another equally handsome man and his three children of varying ages—who had to be royal too—and his beautiful wife. The woman winked at her as she curtsied and whispered in a British accent, 'Keep going, Your Highness, you're nearly there.'

A nervous smile tugged at Orla's lips, but then she rounded the corner, and the smile died.

Her breath caught in her lungs and her steps faltered as her gaze landed on Karim standing at the end of the line of guests.

He stole the last of her breath; his tall, muscular build made even more overwhelming, if that were possible, by the gold and silver robes of the King and the fierce planes and angles of his face only made more dramatic by the ceremonial headdress.

Royalty totally suited him, she thought, desperately trying to tame the giddy leap of her heart and the now flame-grilled dive-bombing butterflies.

His golden eyes locked on her face, then flared with heat as she approached. The weight of arousal dropped deep into her sex and tangled with the stabbing pain of his rejection.

His shoulders tensed, his sensual lips pressed into a firm line and a muscle in his jaw twitched as he reached out a hand and captured her trembling fingers.

'Orla…' he murmured, his voice so husky it seemed to stroke every inch of exposed skin. He blinked as if collecting himself then said so low only she could hear it, 'This won't take long.'

But I don't want it to end.

She stifled the foolish romantic thought.

What was wrong with her? Why couldn't she get this whole thing in perspective? How could she wish for more when she'd always known this wasn't real?

He drew her to his side and folded his arm under hers to hold her steady, as the officiant began to read out the marriage rites. She had been told the ceremony itself would be brief, but somehow she lost track of time, the force of him beside her completely overwhelming her senses.

She couldn't hear the officiant's words over the punch of her own heartbeat. Couldn't smell the delicate garden perfumes of orange and jasmine and rose over the intoxicating musk of man and soap. Couldn't feel anything but the strength of his big body next to hers, his thumb absently stroking her knuckles and making the pounding in her sex painful. And couldn't see anything but the blur of colours through the jewelled veil and the commanding aura of this man who was about to become her husband... And yet not.

After what felt like several millennia, the words she hadn't understood had all been said. Turning, he lifted the veil and she saw the slash of colour highlight his cheekbones before his eyes flared with a fierce longing that detonated in her sex.

He swore—his expression full of frustration—then captured her face in callused palms and bent to cover her lips with his.

Applause and cheering, gunfire and the pop of firecrackers surrounded them, but as he feasted on her mouth, delving deep, the possessive kiss destroyed the last of her sanity. She clung to his waist in a desperate attempt to anchor herself and the only sound she could hear was them both, surrendering to the storm of need.

She wanted this, she wanted him, and God help her that was one thing she couldn't fake.

'Thank you so much for winking when you did. It helped me get the rest of the way down the aisle,' Orla said to the staggeringly beautiful and insanely smart woman she had just been introduced to.

Queen Catherine of Narabia was a British scholar originally, but as she stood next to her husband Sheikh Zane, who had their youngest child on his hip while the other two chased each other in the garden behind them, it was hard not to see how well she had adjusted to life as the wife of a desert king.

Catherine laughed. 'You looked absolutely exquisite but also terrified and I knew exactly how you felt, so it was my duty as a woman to do *something*.'

Orla found herself smiling back, despite the nerves running riot in her stomach. Karim's arm remained around her waist, as it had been ever since their kiss had caused such a stir an hour ago. The heavy weight felt possessive and strangely protective, as he had introduced her to all the guests, but she was brutally aware of the tension rippling through his body, every time she moved. And the thought that this might well be the last time she would ever be this close to him.

'How did you two meet?' Catherine's husband, Sheikh Zane, asked casually. But Orla could sense the intelligence behind his questioning gaze.

Was it obvious, she wondered, how fraudulent this marriage really was?

Ever since the ceremony itself had finished, Karim had made a point of shepherding her around the reception with him, which she had to believe was as torturous for him as it was for her.

He looked drawn, she had discovered, once she'd managed to calm down enough after the ceremony to gather her senses. Not just drawn, but tense and on edge.

'His manservant tells me he does not sleep well at night. That he wakes from nightmares and paces his chamber.'

Orla's heart pulsed in her throat as she recalled what Ameera had told her about Karim's sleepless nights that morning. But the wave of sympathy only made the heat that continued to ripple at her core—every time she got a lungful of his scent—more torturous.

She tried to remember the story they'd worked out to give Zane a coherent answer, when Karim's hand moved to her hip and her emotions cartwheeled into her throat again.

'I bought her family's stud in Kildare. We met while I was considering the sale,' Karim supplied.

'You know about horses, Orla?' Catherine asked, thankfully changing the subject.

Orla nodded, suspecting that Catherine had detected the unease between her and Karim, from the kindness in her eyes, and was trying to alleviate it. Why did that only make it worse?

'Yes, I… I managed the stud for a number of years,' Orla replied. 'Racing and horses are my passion,' she added.

They were putting up a good show. No one need know what was really going on… But still his response to her note tormented her.

Had she done something wrong, by reaching out to him? Was that the real reason why he had decided not to share a bed chamber with her tonight?

'Our daughter Kaliah would love to meet you. She's passionate about horses too,' Catherine added with a gentle smile, as she pointed out the stunning pre-teen girl across the courtyard who was dressed in an elegant trouser suit speckled with mud while she raced around with her younger brother.

'And far too much of a daredevil.' Her father

shuddered theatrically, but Orla could sense the Sheikh's fierce pride in his oldest child.

'Not unlike her cousin Jazmin,' the tall man dressed in magnificent tribal wear who Orla had noticed with his pregnant wife earlier announced as he joined them. He looked slightly harassed, probably because he had one of his toddler daughters perched on his hip—who Orla suspected was the aforementioned Jazmin because she was bouncing up and down shouting, 'Giddy-up, Daddy.' An identical little girl gripped his hand and hid behind his legs.

This had to be the fearsome Chief of the Kholadi tribe, Prince Kasim, known to his friends as Raif, if Orla remembered correctly. Although he looked a lot less fearsome with his daughters in tow.

'Hey, Raif.' Zane slapped him on the back. 'I see you got left holding the babies again,' he added with a smile, before the little boy on his own hip started to chatter to the bouncing Jazmin.

The children were cousins, Orla realised, as she recalled that the etiquette advisor—while going over the guest list with her—had told her the Kholadi Chief Prince Kasim and the Sheikh of Narabia were half-brothers. The man had also mentioned that Queen Catherine and Princess Kasia, Raif's wife, were best friends.

It wasn't hard to tell, as the brothers shared a knowing look while their toddler children jabbered to each other.

These people were family, the unit they made so obviously strong and bonded. The boulder of emotion that had been dogging Orla all day—especially since receiving Karim's note—swelled in her throat. She blinked, trying to control the pain in her eyes.

Don't you dare cry.

But then Karim's hand shifted on her hip again, and the boulder that had been expanding all day settled in the centre of her chest as she glanced up at him. He was staring at her, his gaze so intense, the boulder felt as if it were about to crush her ribs. She looked away, knowing how foolish it was to regret the fact she and Karim would never make a family like the Khan brothers and their wives and children.

Why should that derail her emotions now, when this relationship had always been a business arrangement? This lavish ceremony didn't change that, no matter how significant it had felt as she had walked down the aisle towards him. And he had branded her with that incendiary kiss.

'Has anyone seen Kasia?' Raif's question interrupted Orla's troubled thoughts. His gaze roamed around the garden, his anxiety obvious as he searched for his wife. 'She was only supposed to be going to the restroom, but I think I may have to insist we retire. She looked tired and I don't want her on her feet too long.'

Karim clicked his fingers, signalling a servant boy over. 'I'll have her found immediately,' he said to Raif. He gave the servant instructions. As the boy raced off to do his new King's bidding, Karim added, 'Would you like me to arrange for a nurse to take your children to your rooms and put them to bed while we locate Princess Kasia?'

Raif smiled a warm but weary smile that softened his rugged features and made his eyes glow.

The boulder ripped a hole in Orla's chest.

No man had ever looked at her like that… Except Kasim. But that had always been a lie.

'It's okay, I've got them,' Raif replied. 'We always put the girls to bed ourselves. Can't even imagine what chaos that is going to cause when the next two arrive,' he added with a sigh. 'But I guess we're going to find out pretty soon.'

Two? So his wife was having *another* set of twins. No wonder the Kholadi chief looked so anxious, and his wife had been so enormous.

'Perhaps you should stop impregnating her with more than one baby at a time, then, bro,'

Zane said, the affectionately smug tone getting a rueful eyebrow quirk from his half-brother.

'Don't worry, *bro*. I am not going to let Kasia talk me into impregnating her again *ever* after this,' he said bluntly, before bidding them all goodbye and leaving with his daughters to locate his wife.

A few moments later, a man Orla recognised as one of Karim's many personal assistants arrived and whispered something in his ear.

Karim cleared his throat and nodded, then turned back to her and the Narabian royal couple. 'Apparently the feasting is about to begin, and my...' His gaze locked on her face, the glance so fierce and penetrating she felt the answering tug in her sex. 'And my wife needs to retire.'

'We should leave you to say your farewells,' Catherine remarked, her gaze alight with humour and something compelling that looked like understanding as she touched Orla's trembling hand. 'I'm so glad to have met you, Orla. I hope you can come to visit us in Narabia very soon.'

'That would be grand,' Orla said, blinking back tears again as the royal couple left with their children.

She wouldn't be going to Narabia or anywhere else.

She had been told by the etiquette consultant

she would be asked to leave the festivities early to prepare her for the bridal bed... But Karim had already made it clear he would not be joining her tonight, or any night.

There were so many things she wanted to ask him, she realised. So many things which had been too private to bring up with an audience.

A courtier announced the feasting and the guests began to head towards the palace's banqueting hall—finally giving them a moment alone.

'Why don't you want to join me tonight, Karim?' she whispered, before she lost her nerve. 'Did I...? Did I do something wrong?'

'No, of course not,' he said, but something shadowed his eyes before his face became an impenetrable mask. 'I have arranged for you to return to Kildare in the next few days and the marriage to be annulled in a few months' time.'

'But I thought we'd agreed we wanted to finish what we started?' she blurted out, before she could stop herself. Maybe she had no power to control this relationship at the moment, but if he felt nothing at all for her, why had he brought her with him to Zafar, why had he kissed her with such passion and purpose an hour ago and why had he kept her anchored to his hip ever since?

His eyes flashed with a fire that seemed to

sear her right down to her soul, and his hand gripped her waist for a second, almost as if he were struggling with the same yearning she seemed incapable of controlling, but then he dropped his hand, and his voice when he spoke was rough with command. 'It would only confuse things between us even more, Orla, and you know it. And it could make an annulment more complicated.'

Before she could question him further, demand a real explanation, the personal assistant reappeared with two of the women who had helped prepare her for the ceremony. 'Goodbye, Orla,' he said.

As she was led away, the brutal yearning tore at her insides along with the painful feeling of inadequacy. She forced herself not to look back.

She went through the motions as the women took her to a luxury suite of rooms at the back of the palace that overlooked a secluded courtyard. She was presented with a tray of lavish dishes, some of which she tried to eat, so as not to offend them, but the last thing she felt like right now was food. The women then insisted on bathing her in essentials oils.

Where was Ameera? She wanted her friend here, but at the same time she decided it was probably good she wasn't. Keeping up appearances was the only thing that mattered now.

And holding back the tears that had been building all day.

After the women had insisted on brushing out her hair and dressing her in a ridiculously suggestive diaphanous robe, Orla finally managed to persuade them to leave.

All of this was for show too, she realised, to convince the palace staff this was a real marriage. When it wasn't and it never had been. But as she found the suite's only bedroom and climbed into the huge mahogany bed, she allowed the tears to finally fall.

She didn't even know why she was so upset. Was it the disappointment of a passion unfulfilled, was it the perfunctory note he'd sent her, was it simply emotional exhaustion from the confusion of the last few days and the stress of the ceremony itself, or was it the fact she had somehow ended up investing something in a relationship that wasn't real?

The tears finally stopped as the sky lit up with flares of colourful fire and the distant crackle and pop as the guests finished celebrating the wedding of Zafar's new King and Queen.

When the sky returned to black, she finally sank into a restless and troubled sleep.

CHAPTER THIRTEEN

KARIM DRAGGED OFF the heavy keffiyeh he'd been wearing all day and ran his fingers through his sweaty hair. He dumped the headgear onto the lounging sofa in his suite's bathing chamber, then sat down to yank off his boots, aware of the lingering scent of summer flowers.

Damn it, even her scent is haunting me now.

He threw one boot, then the other across the room, in a vain attempt to use up some of the energy that had been pounding through his veins for four hours now, ever since he had turned to see Orla in the traditional Zafari wedding gown, her curves clearly visible through the gossamer material, her wild hair tamed by sparkling jewelled pins, and her eyes—brimming with awareness and need and understanding—crucifying him.

He tore off his tunic—the vicious arousal still pulsing through him.

By rights he should be exhausted. He'd barely

slept since arriving in Zafar, the nightmares he'd thought he'd conquered so many years ago returning to disturb his sleep each night. But as well as the nightmares there had been dreams of her—his so-called wife—not just her livewire response, her lush curves, the taste of innocence and arousal that had tricked him in the limo so many days ago, but also her smile and those emerald eyes, the same honest green of her homeland.

He shouldn't have kissed her tonight, shouldn't have given in to the urge to mark her as his in front of their guests, because she wasn't his. But something had happened when he'd lifted her veil and she'd stared back at him with a desperate yearning that matched his own—that damn compassion shining in her eyes, which had tormented him and made him weak. And suddenly his lips had been on hers, and her instinctive shudder of surrender had reverberated through his body as he devoured her.

He'd been hard, or semi hard, ever since. Even after she'd left the ceremony—through about thirty courses of rich food, which he hadn't been able to swallow, and almost as many toasts, which he hadn't been able to drink because he knew if he started he would never be able to stop.

He kicked off his trousers and stood naked in

the large tiled room, aware of the bathing pool that had been prepared for him—and the blood coursing through his rampant erection.

What he needed was a cold shower, and to forget her. She would be gone in a few days. He'd already made the arrangements, knew he couldn't see her again or he would break.

He headed into the tiled shower area. Thank God one of his father's many luxury expenditures had included adding state-of-the-art plumbing to the traditional network of pools in the King's bathing suite. He switched the dial down to frigid and stepped in. The needle-sharp spray pummelled his tired muscles and refreshed his sweaty skin.

He wrapped a sheet of linen around his midriff and headed out onto the balcony that overlooked his private gardens. The scent of water tinkling below in the fountains, and the mix of rose and jasmine and white musk from the garden's exotic foliage, permeated the night, but still all he could smell was Orla.

Was he actually going mad? From sexual frustration and the battle to keep the endless thoughts, the desperate need to give her more, to take more, under control until he had finally sent her away? And this painful longing—the terrifying vulnerability that haunted his dreams?

He entered the bed chamber, ripped off the towel, then slammed the door shut to close out the scents of the night garden.

But then he stopped dead, as a figure rose on the bed.

'Karim?' The soft, seductive Irish accent—lilting and confused—was thick with sleep.

His eyes adjusted to the moonlight streaming through the open windows, the light breeze from the desert stirring the still air in the stuffy room. And his flesh stiffened so fast, the vicious pulse of need pushed him towards madness.

She was like a vision kneeling on the bed, her naked body draped in a gossamer veil that caressed her slender curves, framing the flare of her hips, the turgid jut of her nipples, the curls between her legs where he could remember her slick and swollen, and the mass of red hair falling over her shoulders like fire.

His erection turned to iron.

Why is she here? Who brought her to my rooms when I told them not to?

The puzzling questions drifted in and then out of his brain, but he couldn't grab hold of them, didn't care any more about the answers, the wave of need and desire and longing so swift and unforgiving it propelled him across the room towards her.

She was his. And he wanted her. And he

didn't care any more about the consequences. He'd done his best, but he would go mad now if he didn't have her.

He touched her hair as he climbed onto the bed, felt the soft silky strands curl around his questing fingers, then tugged her closer. He cradled her face, tilted her head so he could drown in those fathomless eyes—now dazed with need. He pressed the painful erection into the soft swell of her belly and brought her mouth to his.

'Orla,' he whispered across her lips. 'I need you so damn much. Tell me you need me too.'

It was more demand than question, but he waited—the anticipation building like a volcano—as her wide eyes filled with desire.

'Yes,' she whispered.

It was all the answer he needed as his mouth swooped down to claim hers, and his hands fisted in the misty garment.

He ripped it off her body, the sound of rending fabric joined by the shattered pants of their breathing.

He cradled her breasts, rejoiced in the heavy weight. He rubbed his thumbs across the rigid nipples, the hunger pounding through his veins as he felt them pebble and swell under his touch. He shook violently, determined to savour rather than devour the fragrant flesh he had waited so long to own. He thrust his tongue into her mouth—in deep, demanding strokes—as he cupped her sex at last, trailed his finger through the wet curls and found the proud nub of her clitoris.

She jolted, panting in broken sobs, as her body danced to his touch. Her back bowed, instinctively offering him her breasts.

He worked the spot as he captured one rigid peak then the other and suckled, forcing her to orgasm.

She shuddered and moaned as she crested. And finally collapsed into his arms.

He pushed her down onto the bed.

He couldn't wait a moment longer. The need so fierce, so brutal now he was scared it might rip him apart.

Holding her thighs, he angled her hips and pressed his shaft at her entrance, then thrust deep.

She flinched, as he tore through the slight resistance and plunged into the all-encompassing heat.

Is she...?

The horrifying question formed... But as the wave began to overwhelm him, he let it go, too dazed, too desperate to engage with anything but the feel of her—so hot, so devastating, welcoming him in.

He buried himself to the hilt, moving out and then rocking back, giving her the full measure of him, feeling her milk him as she reached another climax. The battle to hold on, to hold back, became impossible, as the swell of pleasure clawed at the base of his spine.

He flung his head back, shouted out his pain, and poured himself into her—as he surrendered to the exquisite pain. And let himself fall.

Am I dreaming? It feels like a dream. A brutally hot, wild, frantic dream.

As Orla floated down through the blissful cloud of afterglow, the dream turned into something too earthy, too intense, too sore to be anything but real.

The weight of Karim's body pressed her into the linen sheets, his heavy length still stretching her tender flesh. The salty musk of sex and sweat surrounded her. She could still taste the frenzied desperation of his kisses, feel his lips on her nipples, his touch, so sure and perfect, driving her to one titanic orgasm, then another.

The sound of his rough breathing, and the thundering beat of her heart, were deafening. They lay like that for seconds, maybe even minutes, as she tried to hold back the storm of emotion threatening to engulf her.

She'd seen the desperation in his face, heard

the need in his voice, felt the exquisite stab of pleasure combine with the deep well of something she knew she had no right to feel.

The fierce longing contracted around her ribs and she struggled to draw a steady breath. What did this mean? Were they really married now?

Don't be an eejit.

The promises they'd made to each other tonight had all been false. Nothing had changed, not really.

This was just the sex talking. Raw, epic, far too intimate, long-overdue sex, but still just sex.

Karim had been her first. And she'd been fascinated with him for a while now. But sex didn't mean intimacy. Or even affection.

A warm desert breeze played over her skin. She shuddered, aware of her nakedness, and his. He'd torn off the negligee, suckled her breasts, worked her clitoris with a focus and purpose that had shattered her in seconds. The echoes of sensation still caressed her skin. She'd had no time to deal with the emotional impact, but it started to besiege her now.

'Karim?' she whispered into the darkness. He didn't reply.

She slid her palms down his back and realised his rough breathing had fallen into a deeper rhythm.

Was he...? Was he asleep?

She blinked rapidly, aware of the dark silky waves of his hair tickling her nose, and the ridge of his collarbone digging into her shoulder.

She shifted, managing to get her hands underneath his shoulder blade, and gave him a gentle shove.

He rolled off her onto his back. She gathered the thin sheet up to cover her nakedness, aware of the sticky residue between her thighs and the memory of him plunging into her so hard, so fast, so furiously. He was a large man, in every respect, but it had only hurt for a moment. Even so she had seen the stunned question in his eyes, and regretted the lie she'd told him about her experience.

She glanced across at him. His usually harsh features looked relaxed and almost boyish in sleep, the smudges under his eyes shadowed by the long eyelashes resting against his cheeks.

Why had he come to her? Had it been an accident? Had her attendants put her in his rooms by mistake? It had to be so, he had looked as shocked as her, when she'd woken—dazed and disorientated—to find him standing at the end of the bed, so powerful and compelling and irresistible. Everything she'd imagined and a lot she hadn't.

It had all happened so fast, and yet the memories now spun through her mind on a loop. The dance of his tongue, branding her, owning her. The touch of his fingers, finding the heart of her pleasure and exploiting it ruthlessly. The fierce frown on his face as he plunged inside her and made her his.

Except she wasn't his. He was sending her home in a few days. And the only reason this had happened was because the palace staff seemed to have their own agenda, which had nothing to do with what Karim wanted.

She let out a guttered breath, tried to keep a firm grip on the sinking sadness in her heart.

She shouldn't stay in his bed, shouldn't encourage any more intimacy between them. This was about self-preservation now, because she was very much afraid she was falling in love with this taciturn, intense, unattainable man, who also happened to be her husband.

And all that would lead to was devastation.

But as she scooted to the edge of the bed, she heard movement behind her and then a muscular arm banded around her waist and drew her back into the cradle of his big body. She found herself anchored to him, his hot chest pressing against her back, his thighs cradling hers.

He buried his face in her hair, his arm tightening as he held her close—possessive, protective, unyielding.

'Don't…' The gruff words were groggy with

exhaustion but no less demanding. 'I need you... Tonight.'

Just like that her heart tumbled into the abyss. And the tears of misery she had shed earlier turned to tears of tenderness as his breathing descended again into the rhythm of exhausted sleep.

After what felt like for ever, the emotion clogging her throat finally cleared enough that all she could hear was the strong steady beat of his heart at her back—safe, secure, all-consuming—beckoning her into oblivion too.

'No... No... Don't.'

Orla woke with a start, to see dawn lightening the sky outside the bed chamber. The gruff shouts—so full of pain—were echoing in her ear.

Karim.

The events of the night came flooding back, as she became aware of the soreness in her sex, the reddened skin where he had touched and suckled her. And his arm still wrapped around her midriff.

'No... Don't... Don't hurt her.'

She shifted round, breaking his hold. He was still asleep, his eyes squeezed tightly shut, his face a mask of pain, his body rigid with the effort to fight off the dream.

The tenderness that had felled her the night before returned. Bringing with it the deep need to save him from whatever terror was chasing him.

'Karim, it's okay…' She cupped his cheeks. The stubble abraded her palms as he shook his head, attempting to chase away the pain. 'Wake up, Karim,' she whispered fiercely, desperate to free him from the nightmare.

'No…' He gasped, and a tear leaked from his tightly closed eyes. 'Don't. She's crying… You're hurting her.' His voice was raw, deep, but beneath the man's anguish she could hear a child's fear.

This was more than a nightmare. What had happened to him? Who was he trying to protect? Was this why he had needed her so badly the night before, to keep him safe from this?

'Karim, I'm here, you're safe, she's safe, it's okay…' She raised her voice, clung onto his cheeks as his hands curled into fists and she watched him fight to escape the dream.

'No… No…' He tossed his head, the struggle so real and painful, tears rolled down Orla's cheeks too. 'I can't…'

'Yes… You can. It's okay, you can wake up now. Karim?'

His eyelids jerked open, the jagged breaths as he fought to wake making his chest lift and fall in tortured gasps. The shattered depths of his eyes were so full of anguish as he wrenched himself back to the present, a sob caught in her throat. He couldn't see her, not at first. All he could see was the painful memory.

'Karim, it's okay, it's me, Orla. I'm here.' She stroked his cheek, to soothe the hard muscles bunched there. The straining sinews in his neck softened and she saw the moment when he registered where he was, and who he was with, the terror in his gaze becoming shuttered, wary, guarded.

He clasped her wrist, to draw her hand away from his face, then ran his thumb under her eye to capture the last of her tears.

'Why are you crying?' he said, the roughened whisper raw with confusion.

'You... You had a nightmare,' she said, her throat still thick with emotion.

He blinked, and the last of the vulnerability disappeared. To be replaced by something that looked like horror.

He rolled away from her, covered his eyes with his forearm, then swore.

She laid a hand on his chest, felt the harsh tattoo of his galloping heartbeat, the spasms of his breathing still too fast and frantic.

He covered her hand with one of his, the connection arching between them. He still needed her, and she wanted to help. To be here for him.

'Karim, what…what was it about? The nightmare? Do you know?'

He shook his head, his eyes still covered, but he didn't look at her and she sensed it wasn't that he didn't know, but that he didn't want to know.

'You were begging someone not to hurt someone else, a woman, I think,' she managed, knowing she was stepping over that invisible line, again, that barrier that he had erected so deliberately the day before with his note, but refusing to let that stop her. This marriage was more than just a convenience, much more.

She'd left her father to his pain, too scared and insecure to intervene when he'd shut her out repeatedly, and it had been the wrong thing to do. Karim had asked for her help last night and she wanted to give it to him.

'Perhaps if you talked about it?' she began.

'There is nothing to talk about,' he said, his voice strained. 'I told you, I don't know what the damn nightmares are about.' She could hear the lie in his voice, just as she had with her father, when he had refused to confront the pain.

But was he lying to her, or to himself?

'Was it…? Was it your mother?' she asked. His hand gripped hers as he lifted his arm and swung his head round to stare at her—and she could see the horrifying truth in his expression. The truth Ameera had alluded to, the reason why he had struggled so much when returning to Zafar, and why he had talked with such contempt about his father weeks ago, on the day of the ball.

'Did he hurt her?' she asked. 'More than just emotionally?'

His eyes narrowed and he let go of the hand resting on his chest. 'I don't wish to talk about it.'

He whipped the sheet off to climb out of the bed. Heat hit her cheeks at the sight of his naked buttocks, and the evidence, when he turned towards her, that he was fully aroused. The heat gathered in her sex, fast and furious and unbidden as her gaze rose from the hard evidence of his arousal to find him watching her—the answering heat in his eyes as vivid as it was compelling.

'You should go…' he said at last. 'You weren't supposed to be here,' he added, confirming what she'd already guessed, the harsh truth like a blow.

'I know,' she said.

He nodded. 'Then you need to leave now… Unless you want a repeat of last night?'

It was a taunt, plain and simple, a dare, a demand she accept what had happened last night had never been about more than the all-consuming hunger that had blindsided them both. That she had no right to any more of him than he was willing to give her. And she had no doubt at all he expected her to be shocked, disgusted—provoked into letting him scare her away, reduce what they had shared to nothing more than desire.

But it didn't work, because she could still hear the pain in his voice, that strange echo of self-loathing. And she knew what had happened last night hadn't just been about sex, it had been so much more than that, and now she knew why he had tried so hard to diminish and disguise and control what had been happening between them ever since their first night together...

He was scared of this attraction, as much as she was. And she knew, without a shadow of a doubt, however hard it was to confront him, and however vulnerable it made her, one of them had to stop being a coward and admit what was really happening here.

So instead of denying the passion, she took the initiative he had gifted to her last night, let the emotion as well as the desire spur her on and reached for him.

She stroked a finger down the strident erection, rejoicing in the sense of power and connection when it jerked against her touch. And forced herself to say the words she had been denied during their wedding last night.

'I do… Want you.'

And so much more.

'Don't…' Karim grasped Orla's wrist, shocked not just by the fierce passion but also by the brutal tenderness, the unflinching compassion, the unguarded honesty in her gaze—and how much it made him feel.

She knew about what he'd witnessed. How did she know? When until a few seconds ago he hadn't even known himself?

The meaning of the nightmares had eluded him—each night, though, they had become more real, more vivid… The pitiful sight of a woman's body curled into a protective ball, the hollow thud of a man's fists, the terrifying mix of shame and fear and impotent childish rage as he pressed his hands over his ears and cried and begged to make it stop.

But he had been unable to make sense of it, until now. Until Orla.

And now he knew the truth, he was terrified it would break him. The way it had when he was a boy.

'Don't say that unless you mean it,' he managed, his voice raw with need. He would give her the choice. Let her see that he could never give her more than this.

'I do…mean it,' she murmured.

Fire burned through his gut, obliterating the pain and the fear that he had carried with him since childhood. That he would never be whole, never be enough.

He climbed back on the bed, held her wrists above her head, manacling them with one hand. She was at his mercy, her body flushed, waiting, her ripe breasts thrust out, quivering with her need.

Her hair flowed around her on the white linen sheets, the delicate scent of wild flowers and arousal torturing him.

But her gaze—honest, open, unflinching—watched him without an ounce of fear. How could she look so bold, so unafraid, when he was the one in control? And why did he feel so frantic, so desperate, again…?

Once should have been enough to destroy this hunger, but the need was flowing through him like molten lava—demanding he take her again, to escape the pain.

He covered one thrusting breast with his lips, sucking the plump nipple into his mouth, until it swelled and hardened and she shuddered with need. The artless, unashamed response only fired his hunger, his desperation.

He let go of her wrists, let her bury her fingers in his hair as he skimmed his palms down her body, his lips feasting on her and devastating him as she bucked and moaned, unable to hold back. Unable to deny him anything.

He licked at her sex, found the tight nub of her clitoris, feasted on the sweet sultry moans of her surrender until she flew apart in his arms.

He rose above her, the need holding him prisoner. Her gaze—still bold, still unashamed, but soft with a tenderness that terrified him—locked on his. He angled her hips and plunged, burying the massive erection in the tight clasp of her body. He rode the storm, letting it rage around them, cocooning them both in the painful pleasure, the desperate need, and worked the spot he knew would make her fall.

She clasped his shoulders and clung on, her gaze not wavering, not faltering, letting him take his fill—so brave, so beautiful... So his.

Somehow, he held on until the last moment, until she tightened around him.

He yanked himself free with the last of his strength, just in time, to spill himself on the sheets.

Afterglow rushed through his body, but right behind it was the terrible realisation that he'd given Orla something he'd never given any other woman... A glimpse of the vulnerable child who lurked inside him—and would never deserve to be saved.

* * *

Orla held Karim, hugging him, feeling his fear and absorbing it alongside her own. She didn't know what had just happened between them, but it felt so real and significant it hurt to breathe.

She threaded her fingers through his hair, swept it back from his forehead. 'Karim? Are you okay?'

He lifted off her, but his eyes when they met hers were guarded and unyielding. 'Of course,' he said. 'Thanks,' he added, the curt acknowledgement a deliberate blow.

The mask had returned, and her heart ached. But as he threw the sheet back, to climb off the bed, his gaze landed on the sheet beneath her and his whole body stiffened.

His head jerked up and his gaze locked on hers, shocked and accusing. 'Are you on your period?' he demanded.

She could have lied. A part of her wanted to lie. Knowing she must have bled last night and he had spotted the stains on the sheet.

The truth would only make her more vulnerable.

But there were too many lies between them already. Lies and half-truths. And she was tired of trying to maintain them all.

So she shook her head.

He swore and raked his fingers through his

hair. 'So you *were* a virgin last night? You lied to me?'

She nodded.

'Why? Damn it?' he demanded, his face a mask of disbelief, the same horrifying disbelief that had crossed it when he had first taken her virginity.

She clasped the sheet to her breasts and sat up, feeling so exposed now by his searing gaze—which was full of accusation, and even anger.

'Why does it matter?' she asked.

She'd given herself to him, not once, but twice. And she refused to regret it, or apologise for it. The pleasure had been immeasurable, she could still feel the last orgasm rippling through her, but there was a greater significance to what she'd done that she wouldn't hide from.

'Because it gives me a responsibility I didn't want. And you shouldn't want either.'

'What responsibility?' she asked, confused now as well as wary. Why should her sexual experience—or lack of it—have anything to do with what they'd just shared?

'You were untouched, you lied about it, but the consequences are the same. We can't just get an annulment now.' His eyes filled with suspicion and arrogance, and denial. 'If you think you can trick me into intimacy, you're wrong,' he said, his gaze flat and so cold it chilled her to the bone.

The words were like blows, the bitter rejection of what they had just shared hitting that tender part of her heart she'd opened to him. To them.

How could she have been so misguided? she wondered. Karim wasn't a highly strung horse, or a foal just out of its mother's womb. He was a man, who had a great deal more power and experience than she did and that hadn't changed. He might have been vulnerable for a moment, but he didn't want her help.

She couldn't fix his past any more than she could fix her own. And it had been naïve of her to try.

She gathered what was left of her dignity, while her sex was still throbbing from the urgency of his lovemaking, and scooted off the bed.

'Where are you going?' he demanded as she wrapped the sheet around her trembling body and headed towards the bath chamber where the maids had prepared her for his bed last night, without her even realising it. She'd been served up like a sacrificial lamb, and then participated in her own downfall.

You're such a fool, Orla, when will you ever

learn? You can't fix a person who doesn't want to be fixed.

'I'm going to take a bath,' she said, planning to wash and leave as soon as was humanly possible.

His rejection hurt, she realised, but not as much as her own stupidity, because she could still feel the deep pulse of yearning threatening to shatter her heart.

She crossed the large room, desperate to escape as arousal rippled through her traitorous nerve-endings while he donned a pair of black pants. But as she walked past him, he grasped hold of her upper arm.

'We're not finished here. We need to discuss the possible fallout.'

'What fallout?' she asked, as she struggled to hold onto the tears she knew she couldn't shed in front of him without risking the loss of the last thing she had left—her pride.

'You could be pregnant,' he said. His gaze strayed to her belly beneath the sheet, the thickness in his voice something she couldn't interpret. 'The first time... I didn't take any precautions.'

She nodded, her cheeks heating at the memory of that tumultuous joining, all the things she'd imbued it with that weren't real—at least not for him—only damning her foolish heart more.

'It's… It's okay,' she said. 'I wear a contraceptive patch. There won't be any repercussions.'

He frowned, but when she went to tug her arm free, his grip tightened. 'Why do you use contraception, if I'm the only man you've ever had sex with?' he asked.

The heat in her cheeks ignited to sear her chest at the probing enquiry. The personal nature of the conversation felt far too intimate— which was no doubt as ridiculous as the pain in her heart, which refused to go away, given what they'd just shared, not once, but twice.

'I used to have very irregular periods and…' She pushed out a tortured breath. Why was it so hard to talk to him about her menstrual cycle? 'They were very painful. The doctor recommended the pill to regulate them and help with the pain. It worked but I kept forgetting to take it, so I started using a patch.'

It was probably way too much information. But still his eyes narrowed, and she realised he didn't trust her. The irony would have been funny if her heart weren't busy breaking into a million pieces at his cynical expression. How had they come to this?

'I'm not lying,' she said. 'This time.'

Something flickered in his eyes that almost looked like regret, but he let her arm go at last.

As she turned to leave, though, his raw voice stopped her, tight with barely concealed fury.

'If you think you can leave me now, it's too late.'

She swung round, the shattering pain in her heart threatening to consume her. She hadn't wanted to leave him, had given herself to him freely, but he'd taken what she offered, and rejected it. And she could see on his face, that hadn't changed. He was still closed, unyielding, unwilling to bend, unwilling to accept they could have had more.

'I can't stay, surely you can see that?' she said, the battle to hold onto the tears, and keep her voice devoid of the jagged pain now clawing at her throat, making her jaw hurt.

'This is a real marriage now,' he said, his expression tense and wary and utterly uncompromising. 'You don't have a choice, and neither do I.'

CHAPTER FOURTEEN

'WHAT DO YOU MEAN, she's left? Where did she go?' Karim glared at Orla's prim, neatly dressed personal assistant, Jamilla. Unlike his other staff, she didn't flinch instinctively at the sign of his temper, something that for once he found extremely annoying.

He'd given Orla a full six hours to recover from the life-changing events of last night and this morning before having this conversation. But if she thought she was somehow going to avoid the truth by going walkabout in his palace she would soon learn that the power of the King was absolute.

'I don't know, Your Majesty,' the woman said, not even blinking now, let alone flinching…

Karim felt the slow-burning fury—and frustration—turn to something more volatile: panic. 'Isn't it your job to know where she is? You're the Queen's PA.'

'She asked me not to ask her where she was going, so I did not,' the young woman said.

'She…' His glare became catastrophic, but it was the twist of anxiety deep in his stomach that concerned him more. 'She's not in the palace grounds?' The panic rose up to strangle him, the fear more real and vivid than it had ever been in his nightmares. Where could she possibly have gone? They were in the middle of a desert. The nearest town to the palace was over forty miles away. And she had no means of transportation.

'I don't believe so, Your Majesty,' the young woman said. 'She seemed quite distressed when she returned to her rooms this morning,' she added. And he heard it then, the note of accusation, and loyalty.

His temper flared, fuelled by the panic. And the guilt.

He should never have let Orla out of his sight.

He'd needed time to calm down, to deal with the turmoil of emotions that had all but gutted him, while she'd stood in front of him, her eyes full of the pain he'd caused. At the time he'd been furious, convinced her virginity had forced his hand. She couldn't leave Zafar now. Not after last night. An annulment was now out of the question. Because of the Law of Marriage of the Sheikhs, an arcane tradition that had existed in this region for hundreds of years, that stated if a king ever took a virgin to his bed, he must make her his wife. It had all been detailed in their engagement contract, something he was now convinced Orla hadn't actually read.

But once he'd calmed down enough to question his reaction, he'd begun to wonder where that trapped feeling had really come from when he'd spotted Orla's blood on the sheets and realised the truth. Was it really because of an arcane law? When had he ever abided by the laws of Zafar? When had he ever even cared about the country's customs? Or was it because she had blindsided him with her bravery and compassion and the heat that had only got worse each time they had sex?

What had he really been furious about? That he would be forced to make this marriage real, or that he had known, despite everything, he couldn't bear to let her go now?

Was this about her virginity, or was it about his need, the need that had flared and pulsed inside him, a need he'd never even acknowledged existed until he'd met Orla? And the fear he could only ever be whole now with her in his arms?

But he had to find her first to figure out the truth.

The fear that something might happen to her

before he could made the turmoil of emotion tie his guts into knots all over again. He glared at the assistant, satisfied to see her blink at last. He spoke to her in low tones, the menace in his voice a cover for the desperation. 'Where did she go?' he demanded again.

'All I know is that she headed to the stables,' the woman replied.

The stables? The panic swelled and careered into his throat, making it hard for him to breathe, let alone think. He charged past the assistant. He would have to fire her another time.

'Hakim, get to the stables now,' he shouted as he strode into the office next door to his study. 'Have a stallion saddled for me and then speak to the stablemaster… My wife has left the palace on horseback and I need to know where she went. I will meet you there in fifteen minutes.'

'But, Your Majesty—' The young man began, looking stunned.

'Now!' he shouted.

He heard Hakim racing down the palace corridor towards the stables as he took the stairs to his suite two at a time.

Why had he given her time to consider her options? To run away from him? Perhaps because he hadn't really been able to think clearly ever since he'd met her?

He arrived in his chamber and began stripping off the ceremonial robes he'd worn that morning to say goodbye to his official guests.

Thank you for inviting us all to your wedding, Karim. It was wonderful to meet your wife. Orla seems smart and brave, both qualities she will need to adapt to the role of Queen.

Queen Catherine Nawari Khan's parting words—before she and her husband had escorted their children to Zane's waiting helicopter—echoed in Karim's head again as he yanked riding clothes out of his closet.

He'd tried to dismiss the look in Catherine's eyes at the time—full of empathy, but also concern. Had she guessed that he had been using Orla? That he needed her much more than she would ever need him?

Guilt stabbed into his gut.

If Catherine knew, a woman he'd only met a few times, did Orla know too…?

That he simply did not have the courage to let her go. He'd seen the need in her eyes, not just desire, but something more than that, something that had terrified him while also making the yearning to keep her so much worse. And he'd chosen to exploit it.

He should have guessed, though, that Orla was too stubborn and independent—too smart and brave—to settle for his demands. What he hadn't counted on was that she would do something so reckless.

After tugging on his riding clothes, he headed down to the stables.

He had to find her. The panic kicked his heart rate up another notch.

The Zafari desert was a dangerous place, especially at night. And there was less than two hours before sunset.

Orla was his wife now, and his Queen, in every way that mattered, which made her his responsibility—and the sooner she accepted that, the better.

Maybe he could never give her his heart... But she would always have his protection.

He had failed one woman once, and it had eventually destroyed her.

He would not fail another.

Orla huffed out a breath as the beautiful white mare crested the rocky edge of the dune and she spotted the shimmer of water in the valley below.

She tugged on the mare's reins and the horse paused, waiting patiently for her next instruction despite the scent of the water making her nostrils flare.

'Good girl, Sabella,' she said, patting the horse's sweaty neck.

The oasis was stunning, just as Ameera had described it when she had given her directions to it that morning. A grove of palm trees and desert scrubs surrounded a large rocky pool, formed by a waterfall seeping from the rocks.

Clucking her tongue and pressing her heels into the mare's sides, she directed the horse down the rocky slope towards it, knowing she would have been just as relieved to see a puddle after three hours in the saddle.

She shouldn't have left the palace, shouldn't have taken the horse, or the risk that she might get lost in the desert. A desert that, she had soon discovered, was as harsh and inhospitable as Ameera had warned her. But she hadn't been able to stay, had known she needed time and space and distance before she faced Karim again.

As Sabella reached the water, Orla climbed off the mare's back and allowed the animal to stick her snout in the pool, while she tied the reins off on a rock. After taking the last sip from her water pouch, she set about removing the saddle bags filled with the gear she had packed for an overnight stay at the oasis. And then the saddle.

She took care of the horse first, preparing her feed pouch for later and brushing her coat, before tethering her to a cooler spot under the trees. Then she set about putting up the tent and making a campfire in the shade, the water still beckoning.

But with the tough ride now over, the chores failed to provide enough distraction to stop the painful thoughts that had been torturing her, ever since she had walked away from Karim that morning.

'This is a real marriage now...' His words shot through her mind again bringing with them that swift, painfully misguided burst of hope, which had been shattered less than a second later—before she'd even had a chance to acknowledge it, or the terrifying truth behind it—when he'd added, *'You don't have a choice, and neither do I.'*

Somehow she had fallen in love with this hard, intractable, emotionally unavailable man. Who she was now very much afraid could never love her back.

What had happened with his mother...and his father...had scarred him in a way that had closed him off to even the possibility of love.

She couldn't save him if he didn't want to be saved. Trying to make him want her, to make him love her, was a pointless task. All she would end up doing was hurting herself more. She'd realised as much when Ameera had told her about the Law of Marriage of the Sheikhs, and she'd finally understood why he had demanded she stay married to him.

Something to do with her virginity. Nothing whatsoever to do with her, or the connection she'd thought had begun to develop between them.

She needed this time in the desert alone to find the strength, not just to defy him, but to leave him and return to Kildare.

After finally attaching the feed pouch to Sabella's bridle so the horse could regain the calories she'd lost during the arduous—and somewhat roundabout—trek to the oasis, Orla stripped off the dusty riding robes down to her panties and T-shirt.

She stepped into the cool water, aware of the ripple of sensation as she submerged herself, wanting to wash away the feel of his touch on her skin. The feel of him, hard and possessive and hers, inside her body. And yet at the same time not wanting to.

The sun was starting to sink towards the horizon at last, the heat still shimmering in a haze, but what should have been refreshing, rejuvenating, was anything but, the heated, painful memories still bombarding her and making her skin feel achingly sensitive, and her heart shattered.

She ducked her whole head beneath the water, scrubbed her aching body, the tender flesh between her legs that still yearned to feel him thick and firm inside her.

But as her breath got trapped in her lungs she was forced to lift up through the surface. The rushing sound of the waterfall covered the hasty beat of her heart, until she realised the pounding sound was getting louder and closer.

She turned, to see a magnificent black stallion gallop to a stop at the water's edge, and the man astride it—dressed in flowing riding robes—his face marred by a thunderous frown, jump down in one fluid movement and declare in a low voice, husky with barely leashed fury: 'Get out of there. Now!'

Karim.

She shuddered at the temper on his face, but kept her chin firm and her breath even—or as even as she could manage while the emotions she'd come here to suppress raged through her again—as she walked out of the water.

At last she stood on the banks, pushed her wet hair out of her eyes, and realised how far she'd come as his gaze raked over her body, making it flare and spark.

Funny to think that the first time she'd ever seen him she had been soaking wet too. But that anxious, desperate girl was gone. She was a woman now, in so many ways, and she didn't need to be scared of how she felt about him.

'Why did you run?' he said, his voice hoarse with fury… But as her gaze met his, her knees trembled, weakened by the pain she could see shadowing his golden eyes. Pain she realised he could not disguise.

'I didn't run.' She locked her knees. If she showed him a weakness now, she would be lost. For ever. 'I just needed time to think.'

'About what?' he said, the caustic question so ludicrous she almost laughed.

'About everything, Karim. About you, about me.' She jerked her thumb between the two of them. 'About what happened between us last night. And about what has to happen now.'

He stepped closer, his gaze so dark and tortured now she could feel the emotion threatening to overwhelm her. 'I told you what is going to happen now. You'll have to stay…your virginity has a significance that you—'

'I know about the Law of Marriage of the Sheikhs,' she cut him off.

His eyes narrowed. And she thought she might be sick, her stomach turning over with dread. Did he think she had always known, and that was why she'd lied? To force his hand, to make this a real marriage? Didn't he trust her at all?

She had always, always trusted him. Did that

make her a fool? Or did it simply make her a woman in love…with the wrong man?

'If you knew, why did you lie about your virginity?' He bit the words out through gritted teeth, the fury sparking in his eyes, but behind it she could hear his defensiveness, and knew this was about so much more than that foolish lie.

'I lied originally because I was scared you wouldn't want to go through with the engagement,' she said, with brutal honesty. 'And I never thought you would find out the truth.'

'You must have known I would though, once we agreed to sleep together,' he murmured.

And she realised he was still guarding his heart with a fervour she had never even attempted to guard hers.

'Did you think you could trap me into making this marriage real?'

There were a million ways she could defend herself. But all she said was: 'Apparently not, because now I want a divorce.'

She could see she had shocked him, the turmoil of emotions crossing his face easy to read for the first time since she had met him.

'What?' he said, the stunned disbelief making it very clear to her that he *knew*… He knew he had captured her heart—that last night had been about so much more than just sex for her—and he'd planned to use it against her. 'Why?'

She dragged a steadying breath into her lungs, wrapped her hands around her waist, the last of the sunlight disappearing behind the rocks to chill her skin, and gathered the last of her courage. 'Because I love you, Karim. And I don't think you can ever love me back.'

Her declaration—so open, so forthright, so vulnerable—struck him like a sucker-punch to the gut, the bravery and dignity on her face as she offered him her heart simply staggering.

A single tear ran down her cheek, joining the sheen of fresh water making her skin glow in the dusky light.

A part of him didn't want to believe her. Didn't want to accept she had offered him everything. Because then it would require him to admit why he could offer her nothing in return.

But then she swiped the tear away, the courage and determination in that single gesture almost bringing him to his knees, and the truth pierced his heart.

He needed her, he wanted her, he loved her too, body and soul.

It didn't matter that it was too soon, too fast, too terrifying. He felt the ice he'd wrapped around his heart for so long cracking and breaking open inside him, and he knew he couldn't stop it happening any more. Couldn't deny or deceive or hide or escape or fail to confront these feelings any longer. Or he would lose her.

'I'll get dressed and we can return to the palace,' she said.

But as she went to walk past him, he grasped her arm.

'No...' he said. 'Don't...' The words choked off in his throat as she turned, her eyes still so full of the compassion he'd tried so hard to reject. 'I don't want a divorce.'

The look she sent him was full of the pain already tearing him apart. 'It's not enough, Karim,' she said softly. 'I can't stay just because you need me, or you want me, or because of some old law that says you have to keep me as your wife. I need more to make this marriage real. I need to know you are at least capable of trying to love me back.'

'You wouldn't want my love...' He pulled her round to face him, dragged her into his arms, felt her shake, her body so fragile, so slender and yet so strong, so perfect against his. 'Not if you knew.'

She looked up at him, grasped his cheeks, her hands cool against his hot flesh, the shattering tenderness in the misty green destroying the last of the ice.

'Knew what, Karim?'

The sob that had been lodged in his throat

ever since he was a child, ever since that fateful night, when he had let his mother be beaten and done nothing to help, and all the days after, when he had watched her sink into herself and he had been unable to beckon her back, grew so huge it tore into his chest... And finally unlocked the words burning in his throat.

'I don't deserve you. I never could.'

Orla could see the crippling pain, the same nightmare that had haunted him that morning. And all the platitudes she could have told him died in her throat. It wasn't enough to tell him he did deserve her. What she felt for him was new and scary and untried. But she knew it was real. And she knew he could love her too, if only he would let himself be vulnerable.

It was a start, an opening, she'd thought she'd never have, and she needed to be so careful now, not to destroy that fragile seed with her own fears and inadequacy.

'Why do you think that?' she asked, the tears clogging her throat as she stroked his cheeks, the muscles rigid with tension.

He pulled away from her, thrust shaking fingers through his hair, and she knew he didn't want to tell her, from the guilt and shame in his eyes.

'I used you, Orla. All the way along the line.

How does that make me any different from him?' he said, his voice breaking, his chin sinking to his chest. 'He hurt her, and I couldn't protect her.'

'But you were just a little boy,' she said, her heart shattering for that frightened child. 'How could you have protected her?'

'I know but… She never recovered,' he said. 'She was always so sad. I tried to make her happy…' She watched his throat contract as he swallowed, the burden that boy had taken on still weighing him down. 'But I never could.'

The tears ran down her cheeks now. 'That wasn't your job, Karim.'

He lifted his head, his gaze finally locked on hers. 'I can't go through that again. I'm sorry.'

And suddenly she knew why he was so scared to love her. And her heart lifted in her throat. All this time she'd thought he was protecting himself, when what he'd really been trying to do was protect her.

The words Ameera had said came back to her again—*'I think he is not a man like his father—and you are nothing like his mother'*— and at last she knew what to say.

'You're not him, Karim. And you never could be.' He shook his head, but she held on. 'But more importantly, I'm not her.'

His tortured gaze intensified, until she felt it sear her skin.

'I'm not fragile,' she said, because she knew she wasn't, and she never had been. He'd shown her that, protecting her and cherishing her in ways no man ever had before him, even when he didn't want to. 'And I won't break the way she did.'

He swore softly and she saw the moment he realised the burden had been lifted. That what she was telling him was the truth.

He gripped her shoulders, then tugged her back into his arms, hugging her so hard she felt her heart soar.

'That's good,' he said. 'Because if you ever run away from me like that again, I may have to spank you.'

Even though she knew he was kidding, the threat felt somehow erotic as the laugh burst out of her mouth and she struggled out of his arms. 'Good luck with that, Your Majesty.'

His eyebrows rose up his forehead, but then he barked out a laugh of his own, the husky chuckle music to her ears.

'Goddamn it, I love you,' he said, before covering her mouth with his in a harsh, searing kiss.

I know.

She kissed him back with all the new, exciting love in her heart.

As she fisted her fingers into his sweaty hair and dragged him closer to let the soft line of her body mould to the hard, unyielding line of his, she knew this was just the beginning. That they had a long way to go yet. But she intended to enjoy every single hot, exhilarating minute, getting to know this dominant, commanding, overwhelming man—her King, her husband, her lover. While trying to figure out how the hell to be his Queen.

But as he scooped her up into his arms and carried her towards the tent she'd set up in the palm trees her core quickened, and her heart swelled—and she knew she was already Karim's Queen in the only place that really mattered.

Inside his full, open, possessive and wonderfully overprotective heart.

EPILOGUE

One year later

'KARIM, YOU HAVE to let me go, everyone is due to arrive in less than three hours and I've got a million and one things to do,' Orla demanded, going for firm and getting giggly instead when her husband's arms banded around her waist and he dragged her back into their four-poster bed. 'And so do you!' she shrieked, a shiver of excitement rippling through her body as he nuzzled the spot behind her ear he knew was guaranteed to melt every last one of her cognitive braincells.

'Explain to me again,' he murmured, nibbling kisses across her nape and sending more delicious shivers of sensation into her sex, 'why we had to invite Zane and Raif and their wives and their five thousand children to Kildare on our wedding anniversary? When I wanted you all to myself?' he added, still doing diabolical things to her neck.

'Because it's been eight months since we went to Rahim and Omari's naming ceremony,' she said, thinking of Raif and Kasia's identical twin boys. 'And four months since we saw them all in New York. And I miss them.' The families had become friends of both her and Karim, treasured friends. Orla, particularly, had relied on the help and advice of Catherine and Kasia in the last year as she had adapted to her new role as the Queen of Zafar.

These days she and Karim divided their time between the desert kingdom, his house in London and their home in Kildare—which Karim had spent a small fortune bringing back to its former glory, just for her.

She placed a hand on her belly, except it wasn't just them any more.

'Plus I promised Kaliah we'd let her see the stud,' she said breathlessly, attempting to squirm out of his arms as his focussed caresses had the shivers of excitement multiplying.

She really did have a ton of things to do.

But then he placed his hands on her breasts, plucking the nipples the way he knew she loved, and she flinched.

'Hey?' He let her go immediately, and turned

her to face him, the playfulness abruptly gone. 'Did I hurt you?'

'It's okay, Karim,' she said, the concern on his face making her heart melt… As it did on a regular basis, every time he treated her as if she was the most precious thing in the world to him.

He swore under his breath and cradled her cheek. 'Are you sure? You flinched…' he said, the bone-deep concern in his eyes making her realise she was going to have to tell him her news. Sooner rather than later. 'Was I too rough? I'm sorry.'

'No, not at all… It's just…' She hesitated.

She'd wanted to prepare for this announcement. She still wasn't quite over the shock of what she'd discovered yesterday morning herself. They hadn't planned this. Had never even spoken about the possibility. Not yet anyway. Perhaps she should have paid more attention when she'd switched contraception, but she must have slipped up somehow. And so here they were.

And while she was sure he would probably be as excited as she was…*probably*…she really wasn't sure if they were ready.

The last year had been one full of tumultuous choices and decisions, a huge adjustment for both of them. They'd had to make so many big changes already, Karim deciding to remain as King, in a constitutional capacity, while Zafar clawed its way back to full democracy and prosperity. The decision to come back to Kildare during the racing season and the job she had taken in charge of the stud when Carly had been headhunted by another stud… And, of course, the commitment they'd made to each other, to do whatever it took to make their marriage work.

This was going to be another massive change, and, as excited as she was about it on one level, she didn't want it to threaten what they had worked so hard to achieve over the last year.

'It's just what?' he said, dropping his hand to rest on her shoulder, the concern in his gaze intensifying. 'What aren't you telling me?'

She covered his hand with hers, forced a tremulous smile to her lips. 'It's just, my breasts are super-sensitive at the moment.'

'Okay,' he said, still looking concerned. And totally not getting it. 'Are you unwell?' he asked, the concern turning to worry.

'No, I'm… I'm…' *Oh, for goodness' sake, just tell him.* 'I'm pregnant,' she blurted out, past the boulder of anxiety starting to strangle her.

'You're…' His gaze darted down to her belly, her very flat belly, then back to her face. The flush of colour on his cheeks only added to the shock shadowing his eyes. 'You're… You're going to have a *baby*?' he managed. '*My* baby? *Our* baby?'

She nodded, blinking back tears now, the glazed wonder on his face making hope swell right past the anxiety and burst like a firework in her chest.

He's not upset, he's not unsure, he looks absolutely overjoyed.

She laughed as he rained kisses over her face, her hair, her body telling her how excited he was, how proud he was, how he couldn't wait to meet their child...

Then he made love to her, so carefully, so tenderly, cherishing each sigh, each sob, each shiver, drawing out her pleasure until she had to beg him for release. And her heart filled with joy all over again. Everything was going to be wonderful.

Karim lay in the bed a little while later, the afterglow still echoing through his system while he stroked his wife's hair.

'It's all right, Karim,' she murmured sleepily beside him as she snuggled into his arms. 'I still won't break.'

You might not but I probably will.

'You better not.' He let out a husky chuckle, and placed a tender kiss on her forehead, swallowing down the familiar flare of panic.

He loved her so damn much, and in approximately eight months' time there would be two people whom he would have to guard with his life, because he could not afford to lose them.

He shuddered, remembering the two squalling baby boys in Raif and Kasia's arms and the two little girls by their sides at the naming ceremony he and Orla had attended eight months ago.

Dear God, possibly even three people—if Orla has more than one baby.

He wasn't remotely prepared for this, was fairly sure he did not deserve it. He placed a hand on her belly, let the well of love inside him deepen and swell... And forced himself to relax.

Perhaps he could get some tips on fatherhood from Raif and Zane, when they arrived. They seemed to have survived it.

He sucked in a breath and let it out again, then murmured, 'I hope you realise you've totally topped my surprise anniversary gift.'

Orla lifted up, propping an elbow on his chest to grin down at him, not looking remotely remorseful. 'I have? What is it?'

He grinned back at her. 'Not quite as phenomenal as a baby.'

Or possibly two babies! Damn.

She sank down to prop her chin on her folded

hands. 'Really? But close?' she said, excitement and curiosity sparking in her eyes. 'So what is it?'

'That's for me to know and you to find out,' he said, kissing her nose.

He'd had the deeds to the stud put back in her name. So that she—and her sister Dervla—would own it again. He knew she'd be thrilled and humbled and overwhelmed, but not nearly as thrilled and humbled and overwhelmed as he was right now after *her* surprise gift, so it seemed only fair to tease her about it.

He lifted her off him. 'Come on, we need to get up,' he said, giving her a gentle pat on the bottom.

'But, Karim,' she cried as he managed to manoeuvre himself out of the bed. Reluctantly. 'Seriously you're not going to tell me what it is?' she finished with a definite whine in her voice.

'Nope, no time,' he said, his grin spreading when she frowned. 'We've got a million and one things to do before our guests arrive.'

By which time she'd be positively bursting with anticipation and desperation.

Welcome to my world, my darling wife.

* * * * *